DESPERADO
A Mile High Noir

Manuel Ramos

For Grace –
thank you &
welcome to
"Noir" –

Manuel Ramos

Arte Público Press
Houston, Texas

Desperado: A Mile High Noir is made possible through a grant from the City of Houston through the Houston Arts Alliance.

Recovering the past, creating the future

Arte Público Press
University of Houston
4902 Gulf Fwy, Bldg 19, Rm 100
Houston, Texas 77204-2004

Cover design by Mora Des!gn
Cover art by Adan Hernandez

Ramos, Manuel
    Desperado : a mile high noir / by Manuel Ramos.
        p. cm.
    ISBN 978-1-55885-770-4 (alk. paper)
    1. Murder—Investigation—Colorado—Denver—Fiction.
    2. Noir fiction. I. Title.
    PS3568.A4468D47 2013
    813'.54—dc23
                                                    2012043781
                                                            CIP

♾ The paper used in this publication meets the requirements of the American National Standard for Information Sciences—Permanence of Paper for Printed Library Materials, ANSI Z39.48-1984.

13 14 15 16 17 18 19 20   10 9 8 7 6 5 4 3 2 1

This book is dedicated to Genaro "Henry" "Hank" Ramos
1928–2012

ACKNOWLEDGEMENTS

Many people contributed to the creation of this book. Some may not realize their role. Each was important to the process. My thanks to all who played a part. These include fellow writers Lucha Corpi, Sarah Cortez, Sandra Dallas, Diane Mott Davidson, Tim Z. Hernandez, Michael Nava, Emma Pérez, Gary Phillips, Catherine Rodriguez-Nieto; family and friends Neil Gotanda, Mercedes Hernández, Florence Hernández-Ramos, Diego Ramos, Maria Santos; my pals at La Bloga; my colleagues at Colorado Legal Services; artist Adan Hernández; and, of course, the great Arte Público staff.

Special thanks to my agent Toni Lopopolo, who took a chance and hung in there.

Thank you

Author's Note

Chapter 5 previously appeared as the short story "The Skull of Pancho Villa," in a slightly edited version, in *Hit List: The Best of Latino Mystery,* edited by Sarah Cortez and Liz Martinez (Arte Público Press, 2009.)

She tried to wash away her sin
with holy water, then covered her body
with a long, thick cloth
so you would never know
her brown skin had been damned.

—©Lucha Corpi (from "Marina Virgin" in *Palabras de mediodía/Noon Words*) used with permission of Lucha Corpi and Catherine Rodríguez-Nieto (translator)

I got to keep movin'
blues fallin' down like hail
And the day keeps on worryin' me
it's a hell hound on my trail
hell hound on my trail.

—Robert Johnson (from Hell Hound On My Trail)

Juan Diego unfolded his white tilma, where he had the flowers; *and when they scattered on the floor, all the different varieties of* *rosas de Castilla, suddenly there appeared the drawing of the pre-* *cious image of the ever-virgin Holy Mary, Mother of God, in the* *manner as she is today kept in the temple at Tepeyac, which is* *named Guadalupe. When the bishop saw the image, he and all who* *were present fell to their knees. She was greatly admired. They arose* *to see her; they shuddered and, with sorrow, they demonstrated that* *they contemplated her with their hearts and minds. The bishop,* *with sorrowful tears, prayed and begged forgiveness for not having* *attended her wish and request.*

—Taken from a version of the *Nican Mopohua* written in Nahuatl by Antonio Valeriano in the sixteenth century.

PROLOGUE

The Basilica of Our Lady of Guadalupe in Mexico City, a combination of tourist destination and sacred church, did not use metal detectors or other screening devices. Guards did not search any of the thousands of daily visitors, and the administrators of the place admitted they had no organized system to prevent an attack. A few soldiers paraded around the grounds with guns, but they primarily snapped pictures at the request of visitors, using the tourists' cameras. The light security contradicted the importance of the basilica's most valuable possession: the blessed tilma of San Juan Diego, the tattered maguey cloak with the Virgin's image imprinted on it, miraculously preserved for more than 400 years, suspended behind an altar where it received believers' prayers and adoration.

When the thieves came, some of them dressed as priests. Others looked like tourists or office workers on break. They smuggled weapons under their coats and jackets. At a pre-arranged signal from one of the leaders, the men opened fire, indiscriminately, trying to panic the visitors. Hundreds of people rushed to the exits. In the midst of the chaos, an explosion ripped through the building. The moving walkway screeched to a stop. A trio of gunmen jumped over the walkway and, using ropes and grappling hooks, secured the frame that held the tilma, bolted high on the wall. They wrenched the frame from its anchors. Pilgrims and worshippers screamed in agony, desperation and fear.

A priest rushed to stop the men. Several of the gang shot him repeatedly. He bled to death crawling toward the altar.

The tilma, frame and glass crashed to the floor, missing by inches the men who hauled it down. The man who had signaled for the raid to begin picked shards of glass from the icon. With automatic weapons exploding around him and men and women screaming and crying, he cut the cloth from the broken frame with a long-handled knife.

He stuffed the cloth into a thick leather case. The gang ran out of the church to a waiting helicopter that sat on the vast plaza surrounding the basilica. The man with the tilma leaped into the helicopter. The other men ran furiously to the fence that surrounded the compound. A few fell, shot by the soldiers or the police who had finally arrived on the scene. Those who made it through the fence jumped into waiting vans that sped off and raced through the streets of Mexico City, headed in different directions.

One of the escape vans collided with a Volkswagen taxi. All of the men in the van and the taxi driver were killed when a rain of bullets from the pursuing police ignited a gas tank and both the van and VW erupted in flames. Meanwhile, the helicopter rose and disappeared into the smoggy Mexico City sky.

A day later the Archbishop of Mexico City received a demand for one hundred million dollars, the release of twenty-five members of the Rojos held in various Mexican prisons and five more doing time in Texas jails. The neatly typed note warned that if the demands were not met, the cloak would be burned and the entire world could watch the venerated object go up in smoke, all played out on the Internet.

Summer in the city. For a few, living came easy. For others, living ended.

I moved to familiar rhythms embedded in memories of days that stretched forever and nights filled with promise. I executed rituals meant to define my existence. I hoped for one more grand time, one more forever. But the sun drove parasites and pests from the shadows and exposed the limits of my hope.

Dry winds rolled in from the mountains and whipped up dust devils on the horizon. Urban grasses and flowers yellowed in the heat. Aged elms and oaks bowed to thirst. When the dog days arrived, monsoon rains filled gutters and drains but failed to clean the city, or me. I struggled like a fish trapped in a net. I searched for a way out, an escape. . . .

1

He looked as cool as ever. Clothes, hair, attitude. Same old Artie Baca—the hippest guy in high school and now coming across like a GQ cover boy, Chicano style. Sharp-creased slacks, form-fitting silk shirt. Reminded me of that song about werewolves in London. His hair was perfect. He had it working that day.

We sat on opposite sides of a metal card table on uncomfortable wooden chairs painted a disturbing bright red. I hadn't dug out the floor fans from the storage room, so the recent heat wave left Sylvia's Superb Shoppe stuffy. Even Mr. Cool had a few drops of sweat on his upper lip. Mustiness surrounded us.

I transacted business at the table when the rare customer bought any of Sylvia's second-hand junk, what she called antiques. I rang up sales on an ancient cash register, accepted cash or ran credit cards, handed out receipts and change, provided bags when necessary and updated the inventory on a laptop. Highly-skilled, no?

The store had large windows through which I watched the traffic on Thirty-Second Avenue. They also magnified the outside heat or cold and were always in need of a good cleaning, as Sylvia reminded me almost every week.

"I need help, Gus." Artie's voice wasn't what I remembered, not as deep. "I don't know who else to ask. It's not something I can talk about to just anyone."

A thin smile and a subtle wink. Yeah, except for the voice this was the Artie Baca I remembered from my less-than-memorable high school years. I hadn't seen him all that much since we graduated—I never made it to the tenth-year reunion—but here he sat, asking for something in that way he had that came off as though he were doing me a favor just by asking. He did that all through North High and got away with it. Almost everyone liked him, some even loved him. I was more in-between ignore and hate. He was a pal, don't get me wrong. At least, that was what I told anyone who asked.

"What kind of help, Artie?"

"This stays between us." The clipped words rushed from his mouth. "You can't tell anyone, not Sylvia, no one. Okay?"

Why would I tell my ex anything? But I let it slide. He had my attention, for sure.

"Whatever, dude. Unless you've killed someone and you want me to get rid of the body, I won't talk to anyone about what you say. No need to."

The skin around his eyes twitched when I said "killed someone" and the healthy tanned hue of his face faded a bit.

"No. Nothing like that. It's about a woman."

That didn't surprise me. Artie copped more tail in high school than the entire football team put together. Girls acted like robots around him. He'd say "Good morning" and they'd drop their panties and bend over. Really, it was almost that bad. Of course, that meant he often hid from one girlfriend while he fooled around with another. Plus, he had more than his fair share of run-ins with angry fathers, brothers and cousins. I said *almost* everyone liked him. He took the hassles in stride—called it "poon tax." "I got punched out by Gloria's brother—paid the poon tax," he'd say, and then try to laugh. It never sounded like a laugh to me, more like a half-assed giggle through clenched teeth. He could be coarse like that, but we were high school kids.

"Aren't you a little old for women problems, Artie? I thought you were married? What happened to that?"

"No, no. I'm married. Linda's a wonderful woman. I got a couple of kids almost in high school. I . . . " His voice trailed off. I filled in the blank spots.

"But one night, probably in a bar, you forgot all about your happy marriage and your kids almost in high school because the young woman flirting with you had beautiful eyes and a pair of chi chi's like . . . "

"Okay, okay," he said. "I screwed up. Bad. I admit it. You don't know how sorry I am that I let it get out of hand. But this was the only time I did anything like that since I got married. I love Linda. I wouldn't hurt her. I just screwed up. One time, and now it's like I'm in hell. This girl is crazy."

"You get her pregnant?"

"Not that, thank God. She wants money, but not for a kid. She's trying to get what she can out of me. It's classic. She said that for ten thousand I can have peace of mind for the piece of ass. That's the way she put it. She'll go to Linda if I don't pay. She set me up. We were both kind of drunk, at least I was, and I let her, uh . . ." He couldn't finish. He pulled out a pocket comb and ran it through his hair. A quiver of nostalgic regret ran through me. I could've been standing in the high school hallway next to my locker, waiting for Artie to set the agenda for the day.

"What happened?"

"I didn't know what I was doing. We was just partyin'. I didn't think . . ."

He caught his breath and turned away when I tried to look him in the eyes. He opened his expensive phone and tapped a few icons. He showed me the video. They were naked on a rumpled bed. A hardcore sex scene that I didn't want to see played out before me. I said, "A sex tape? Really?"

"This could end my marriage," he said, the words dull and flat. "I have no choice. I'll pay her the money."

I almost laughed out loud. The coolest guy in the world became the victim of the oldest con in the book. I stifled my laugh, sat up and tried to sound sincere.

"Wow, Artie. That's crazy. You hear about this kind of stuff, but you never expect that it'll happen to someone you know. A scam out of something like a detective movie, blackmail, who knows what else. What you gonna do?"

"That's why I'm talking to you."

I thought about all the options that he could be referencing. I started to feel uncomfortable with where the conversation with my old high school buddy was headed.

"You want me to lend you money?" I calculated that this was the least disagreeable of the ideas he might have floating around in his head.

He gave me one of those *as if* looks and I felt insulted.

"No, no. I got the money," he said.

At this point I started to re-think my relationship with Artie Baca. I sat upright and leaned forward. We did stupid things in high school and for a year or so after. Typical teenage antisocial behavior and other messes not so typical. The kinds of things that might make him think I'd be up for taking care of a blackmailer. But that wasn't me, never had been. I couldn't be the muscle on a job if my life depended on it.

I should have had a better understanding of Artie, but I relied too much on memories and the secrets we shared, and, well, things went the way they went, all crazy and weird. After it played out, when the dust settled, as they say, I finally realized that I never caught on to his trip, and that turned out to be a big mistake for me, for Artie, for everyone involved.

"I want you to give the money to her," he said. I eased back against the inflexible chair.

"Uh, you should take care of that yourself. Why get someone else involved? Already I know more than you want me to know. Why'd you come to me anyway?"

Artie Baca's lazy eyes finally looked back at me. The girls called them bedroom eyes, but for me they came off as droopy. More sluggish than sexy.

"Insurance. I'm thinking that when this chick sees that someone else knows about her blackmailing, that will be the end of it. You're like a witness. If I'm not afraid to tell you, then she'll understand that the ten grand is all she's getting out of me. One payment and only one or I go to the cops with you as back up. I'll explain it to her so she gets it. But I want you to deliver the same message, along with the money. You don't have to get physical. I'm not asking that."

"You want to put me out there, as your insurance? You ever think she might resent my butting into her action? What if she's not alone, which she probably is not by the way, and her partner decides that there's one too many witnesses and figures he'll eliminate the risk? What if he wants to cancel your so-called insurance?"

He shook his head. "Nothing like that will happen. She's after quick money. Thinks I'm an easy mark. She was stuttering and nervous when she talked to me on the phone. There's no weight behind her. No one else involved. She had a good time with me, then a day or two later it probably sunk in that the rent was due, or that she wanted to enroll in hairdresser college after all. So she started thinking about how easy it would be to make a little something off me. She called me at my office and gave me her pitch. I couldn't believe it. I tore into her, chewed her ass out. She ended up crying and I thought that was the end of it, that I had scared her off. But then she sent me the video and I knew this was serious." He sounded pathetic, looked worse. "I gotta pay her and get this done."

Years of resentment steamed up my throat. "Why in the good goddamn would I help you?"

He tightened his lips into a thin line. His Adam's apple moved up and down. His expensive shirt had a stain near the collar. The Artie I once knew never paraded in public with less than an immaculate presentation.

He reached into the back pocket of his pants and I stiffened. Had I come on too strong? Artie had a violent streak. I'd seen him explode more than once when someone pushed him. He showed me a soft-looking tan leather wallet. An embossed letter "B" stood out on the cowhide. He unfolded a check, and laid it on the table so that I could read it. *Pay to the order of Gus Corral the sum of one thousand dollars and no cents.* No sense. That's me. I should have ripped up the check, told Artie I'd see him around, maybe at the twentieth-year reunion.

"Don't take this the wrong way," I said, almost pleasantly. "I could use the money. But I need to ask again. Why me? It's not like we're BFFs or whatever they call friends these days. I haven't seen you since . . . uh, well, for years. Why me?"

Artie stood up, his six-foot frame still thin and wiry. He paced around Sylvia's dusty shop. He blew his nose into a monogrammed handkerchief.

"Honestly? I think you're the kind of person I need for something like this." I shook my head. He held up his hand, signaling me to calm down. "Don't jump to conclusions," he said. "Nothing negative, Gus. Not like the old days. I considered the cops, but that would mean public exposure. It would make the papers and the TV news. My business would take a hit. I figured ten thousand wouldn't break me plus I could save my marriage and my business. But I needed a guarantee that the woman wouldn't bother me again. I thought about a private investigator, maybe an ex-cop. I wasn't sure there were any of those guys around yet, but I found a few. They're mostly process servers or skip tracers, not really investigators, not someone I'd trust with the money and the secret. A couple were nothing but fat slobs without an ounce of intelligence. Or con men pitching their own grifts. I thought over the people I knew, someone who could be useful in this kind of thing. I remembered what we did in high school, and after. Maybe you didn't know it, but I always thought I could count on you. I could rely on you to do what you said you were gonna do. All the guys thought of you that way. I don't know anyone else, to be frank. I can't go to my lawyer or my business partners. No one."

He stopped talking. When I didn't say anything he must have concluded that he hadn't convinced me yet.

"And, yeah, I figured you could use the money. I heard about you and Sylvia, losing your job, working and living here, all of it. I kept coming back to you. That's why I'm here."

The BS was thick. I knew better than to believe Artie's rap. But I was sure that his check was good. The guy had money. I didn't.

"You have to help me, Gus," he said. "I can't do this by myself."

Those two short sentences carried more impact than his story about his one-night fling, the blackmailing, even that he was willing to pay off the chippie. Artie Baca, begging for my help. I should have felt good about that, I should have stood up and crowed like a rooster at dawn, but all I felt was sadness for something that slipped away from both of us that warm afternoon.

2

Artie's post-high school life could be summarized as a quick evolution from conscienceless Romeo to real estate magnate, with very few stops in-between. When we quit carousing together —a very physical arrest and a month in City Jail will do that for some people—he worked for old man Abel Sánchez back when Sanchez was one of the few Latino realtors in the city. Artie turned a small real estate office into a major enterprise. When Sánchez retired, Baca took over the business and continued to build it with his charm and force of personality. Those were the days when real estate was still a good bargain on the North Side, when old houses could be picked up for a song and then sold to future-thinking developers who saw more happening, eventually, on the North Side than any of us long-time residents could imagine. When the neighborhood started to gentrify, Artie was the man of the hour. By the time the North Side had morphed into "Highlands" he'd sold off several properties at double and triple what he'd paid for them, and he even inserted himself into some of the deals that turned one-family homes into multi-unit condos and townhouses. He made a killing on real estate although in other parts of the city that market went south with the rest of the economy, which meant that one thousand dollars wasn't all that much to him and, apparently, he could also afford ten thousand for a one-night stand that had turned into his biggest nightmare.

I reflected on my circumstances. The recession hit me hard, like everyone else in my family, but at least I had a job, managing my ex-wife's segunda on Thirty-Second. Six days a week, from opening at nine in the morning until I decided to close up, usually around five or six. I pretended to be the night watchman so I could sleep in the place. In the back room I kept a small refrigerator, microwave, toaster oven and a TV that worked most of the time. I had carved out a cozy set-up.

Sylvia provided a cot but she never acted civil to me, even when she dug into the cash register and calculated my weekly pay. The good part was that I didn't have to pay rent. The bad was that I saw Sylvia several times a week when she walked in with her usual scowl and bad attitude. Checking on me, of course. I waited like a hungry dog to get my pay each Friday. But I needed the job. My life hadn't exactly panned out the way I thought it would when I was voted in high school as The Most Likely to Retire Early. Maybe I was retired and didn't know it.

"How were you thinking this would go down?" I said.

"It's simple. She wants to meet so she can get the money. I'll set that up but tell her you'll be there in my place. If she doesn't go for that, I'll play along that I'll be there, too, even though I won't. I don't want anything more to do with the skank. She said she'd give me the video when she gets her money, but you know that doesn't mean anything. She'll have the damn tape forever. I can't do squat about that."

"That's not much of a plan," I said. "I don't really see how my involvement takes care of your problem." I did my best to point out the flaws in Artie's thinking even though my eyes kept returning to the check lying on the table.

He sat back down across from me and picked up the check. "It's all I can do. It'll work. She's weak, over her head. I'd deal with her in a different way except that I'm trying to limit my exposure. If you won't do it, I'll look for someone else. I know a few guys who might . . ."

"I didn't say I wouldn't do it." Artie had a bad habit of jumping to conclusions, of shooting first and asking questions later. He dropped the check on the table. "But I have to level with you. I don't think it'll fly. She'll be back in another month or two, wanting another ten grand. Then again in another six months, for twenty thousand."

He looked lost in his own thoughts. I wasn't sure he heard any of my words.

"If this is how you want to play it, no skin off me, right?" I said. "There's a risk, but the thousand dollars covers that. If you have to pay her again, my delivery fee doubles, simply because I told you so."

"This will work," he said. "It has to. There won't be any next time or any more delivery fees. Our business partnership ends after you take care of this. You can bet on that."

My brain screamed at me to say no. Why get involved with Artie Baca again, after all the years and our bleak past history? But my empty checking account said something else.

I reached for the check but he beat me to it. "You get this when the job is done, Gus. That's how it has to be." He folded the check and slipped it back in his wallet.

"Her name's Misti Ortiz," he said. "That's what she's using anyway."

"Very pop culturish," I said. "Tell her to meet me at Chaffee Park. It's open, more or less, so I can see whoever's coming. The surrounding houses might discourage any rough play. I'll get there early and scope it out. If anyone's with her, I'm out of there. You'll have to go to Plan B, whatever it is."

"I don't like it," he said.

"You don't have a choice."

He twisted his right hand around his left. "I guess that's everything. I'll call you when I confirm the day and time, hopefully today or tomorrow. Then I'll swing by with the cash." He quit twisting his hands and clenched them together while he thought over what he was doing. The sweat had moved from his lip to his entire face. "One more thing."

He produced an obvious computer-generated photograph from his pocket and handed it to me.

"Her picture, so you can be sure you're dealing with the right bitch."

The close-up from the video featured Artie and the woman, cheek-to-cheek, with big, bright, boozy smiles. The girl's bare shoulders hinted at nakedness but there was nothing particularly scandalous about the pose. She had short black hair; a silver ring pierced her left eyebrow. Her glazed eyes focused on a point a few inches above the camera. Dark, near-purple lipstick smudged her mouth and Artie's neck sported a smear of the same color. Artie did indeed look drunk—his eyes were almost closed and his cheeks gave off a reddish glow.

"She from the States?"

"Mexico. Probably illegal. Maybe I can get her deported. Send her sweet ass back to the motherland." He laughed.

I didn't.

I looked at the photo, then Artie, back to the photo. I remembered that Artie was not one of my favorite people and that he deserved whatever grief the young lady wanted to give him. I thought of our past times together, our secrets and our potential for damaging one another. I thought about the check resting in Artie's wallet.

"Okay, Artie. Let's do it."

3

I finished my third cup of coffee and second blueberry cereal bar. A typical breakfast. The wall clock chimed ten times. Forty-eight hours after Artie's visit, I looked out on another pleasant day. The Colorado summer could disappoint a person who didn't like unfailing sunshine or afternoon showers that cooled off the parched air after work.

Work. What a concept. I needed work. I wanted a paycheck in return for my sweat but no one wanted my sweat. I didn't have a choice except to do my time in Sylvia's store. No options presented themselves and my brain refused to produce ideas.

Daily life in Sylvia's Superb Shoppe fluctuated between monotonous and really monotonous. I did what I could to make the routine more interesting. Difficult to do since all I had to work with were second-hand clothes, junk, boxes of frayed baseball cards, chipped porcelain angels and more junk. One man's trash is another man's treasure, except that no one had unearthed any treasures in Sylvia's Superb Shoppe.

Not that people didn't come looking. The typical looky-lou who wandered into the store had recently moved into the North Side, which was happening by the droves over the past year or so. Usually a couple bubbling over with excitement about exploring their new neighborhood, maybe carrying a baby in one of those rug rat slings, most likely leading a big dog that they tied to the bike rack anchored on the red flagstone sidewalk. These folks might buy a coffee cup with a silly slogan or maybe one of the Gold Medal paperbacks that I "gave" to Sylvia when she threw me out. Once in a great while I sold an ugly painting of a horse running in the wind or dogs playing pool because the couple wanted the frame.

Sometimes I was entertained by the guy who watched too much Antiques Roadshow, or the woman who read in the *Enquirer* about someone who found a long lost art masterpiece at a yard sale. These types would look at everything in the store, handle several pieces and whisper to themselves or the person who had tagged along on the scavenger hunt. Eventually, they would leave without buying anything. Sylvia's stuff, no matter how superb, did not excite these people—they saw no potential fortune in the rooster and hen salt-and-pepper shakers or the jars of buttons.

The third type of customer, often an older woman, sincerely looked for bargains. Shoes for the kids or grandchildren, work shirts for the old man, plates for the cupboard, scissors, knives or a hat for herself. I liked these people. They needed what they bought and more than once I gave them a discount on Sylvia's exaggerated prices. Sometimes I didn't ask for any money. Sylvia would have ripped out my eyeballs if she knew, but I made sure she never had a clue.

These customers showed up less and less. I guessed they moved to cheaper housing in another part of town, or the economic crisis made even a trip to the second-hand store a luxury that had to be put off until times got better.

Occasionally someone I knew stopped in the store. Depending on who it was, the visit could be a pleasure or an embarrassment. I experienced both when an old crush dropped in one afternoon.

At North High School, Isabel Scutti and I never connected in any meaningful way. In the early nineties the Italian students didn't mingle much with the Chicano students. The anti-Columbus protests that rocked Denver every October chilled cross-cultural fraternization. Each group agitated about cultural and ethnic pride. Phrases like "genocide" and "freedom of speech" were casually thrown around. They lost their impact, but lines were drawn and not too many of us crossed them. But that didn't stop me from daydreaming about Isabel. Can't say now what the big attraction was back in high school, but when she walked in the store I stared for too long, then tried to smile, then blurted out, "Isabel! Look what the cat drug in."

She frowned. "The cat?"

"Sorry. Guess I'm surprised to see you, that's all."

The frown turned to a smile. She looked me over, conducting her own inspection of the weirdo in the second-hand shop. "Gus Corral. I thought that was you. It's been years." Years that hadn't aged her at all.

I knew bits and pieces of her history. Her family lived in the North Side for eighty years or so. A great-grandfather came over from a Sicilian village. A few branches of the Scutti family continued to live in or near the old man's house on Vallejo Street, although many of their fellow Italians moved away. She graduated from the University of Northern Colorado and I'd heard she taught at Horace Mann, still on the North Side, and published a trio of poetry books. Never married but she had compiled a long list of ex-boyfriends. That last according to my sister, Corrine, who periodically filled me in on the adventures and misadventures of our classmates.

"Yeah, years. You look the same. Like you just turned in your paper in Advanced English and expect an A."

"I promise I'm not looking for answers to the Algebra homework. That's what I always seemed to bother you about."

She stayed only for a few minutes, and we didn't really catch up. We never advanced beyond the light and pointless banter stage. After she left, I wanted to listen to do-wop and drink beer. I wanted to slow dance. I wanted to cheer at a football game and hold hands in study hall. Truth be told, I wanted to wallow in all the "might-have-beens" that I could imagine, and I had dozens of those.

When I wasn't clicking through the Internet on Sylvia's computer or dealing with the occasional customer, I sat at my table reading paperbacks, some for the third or fourth time. I listened to music on an old CD player I borrowed from Sylvia's inventory. Bob Marley. Los Lobos. Stevie Ray Vaughn. Oldies, but that's what the customers brought in. I paid two dollars for ten used CDs and sold them for fifty cents each. Second-hand capitalism.

Or I thought about how I screwed up my marriage to Sylvia. I spent hours doing that. Made me a real fun guy to be around. We never got along, even when we dated. Two different people, completely. Why we got married, only the devil knew since he had to be the one who hooked us up.

Who was I kidding? The answer was S-E-X. We argued constantly but we made up passionately. On the good days, and I admitted that there had been plenty of good ones, we couldn't keep our hands off each other. We had marathon sex. Quickie sex. Afternoon sex. Wake up at midnight sex. Do it in the backseat of our car while it was parked in the driveway sex. Our lifestyle of sex and more sex lasted a few years until we finally burned out.

We made plenty of love but we never made peace.

When we divorced she took everything—house, car and computer—and left me the bills. After my delivery gig tanked and my boss laid off me and everyone else, she graciously hired me to be her grunt, delivery boy, all-around slave. She thought it was funny that her ex-husband worked for her. Sylvia had a mean sense of humor—hell, she was plain mean.

In addition to the shop she earned money as an office temp, filling in for vacationing secretaries or flu-stricken receptionists, and she actually had a pretty good thing going as a consultant, for anything from starting a company to managing office human relations. She also inherited a nice chunk of change from an aunt, I never knew how much for sure, but she could count on a monthly check from a lawyer somewhere in Texas. Each month that check paid for new shoes and regular hair and nail updates—the essentials as far as she was concerned. The aunt died after our divorce became final, naturally.

Sylvia wasn't all that deep. Sexy, yes—when we got married. She let herself go a little after we broke up. Her business savvy, or luck, turned out to be her best asset. She certainly lived better than me. The neighborhood politicos looked to her as a leader of the community, not because of her brains or knowledge but because she could be counted on for hard work and connections. They appointed her to committees and task forces as the voice of the

Latina business person. Flash and glitz but no substance, in my opinion. Maybe I was biased.

I turned on the CD player.

At the three-quarter hour mark, my curiosity got the better of me. I stopped ignoring the photograph that I stored in a cigar box I'd saved from Sylvia's trash. I examined the picture of Artie and the girl several times and each time something nagged at me.

I guessed that Misti Ortiz was in her early twenties, but I couldn't be sure, not from the photograph. The silver ring in her eyebrow had a tiny dot of turquoise that I'd missed when Artie gave me the photo. Unlike Artie, her eyes were wide open—glassy for sure, but open. The images were fuzzy, so what looked like a bruise on her shoulder could have been a tattoo, or dirt. I rummaged through the store for a magnifying glass to help me see the details better.

I found a pair of pink reading glasses. They were too small for me and they fit tight around my face but they did the job. I balanced them on my nose and didn't hook them behind my ears. I slouched over the table and bent close to the photograph. I stared at the bruise or tattoo or dirt.

"What're you looking at?"

I jerked backwards and the glasses rolled off my face and clattered on the floor.

"Damn, Sylvia, you scared the hell out of me."

She picked up the glasses from the floor, wrinkled her nose and shook her head. She did it slowly and with such sadness that I started to feel sorry for myself. That's the effect Sylvia had on me. I think she purposely snuck in the back door and didn't make a sound so that she could see for herself whether I was stealing the "thousands of dollars" that the store had to be earning each day.

She put the pink glasses on the table and grabbed the photograph.

"Who's this? Can't be one of your girlfriends, she's too cute. And this guy. Who is he? I kind of recognize him." She stretched her arm and held the photo away from her. "Is that Arturo Baca?

He's smashed, nothing new about that. The girl? Way too young for him. Looks like they're good friends. His wife know about this?"

If Artie expected me to keep his confidences, Sylvia blew them wide open, without trying. She immediately guessed the basics of the sordid tale Artie told me including the part that Artie's wife would not be happy with the photograph.

I snatched back the incriminating picture.

"Artie stopped by the other day and left this by accident." My brain clutched for straws. A lie had to be better than the truth. "I don't know anything about it except that Artie had it. Don't jump to conclusions."

"Still covering for him? Just like high school. Gus, you'll never learn."

"Don't start."

I knew she was right but I'd never say it. I never said I was sorry for messing around on her, either, and look what that got me. Sex brought us together, and sex drove us apart.

She shrugged. "Nothing new, I guess."

She stepped back from the table and inspected me like a dress on Nieman Marcus' rack. "I told you to clean up your act. No more jeans, T-shirts or muscle shirts. You don't look good in those clothes. You don't have any muscles, for one thing."

I wore a wife-beater but I didn't think I needed to correct her on that point.

"Your hair, my God." She was relentless. "It's so short I can see the veins in the top of your head. Masquerading like a gangster will drive away the customers. Your hoodlum haircut and those mirror sunglasses give people the wrong idea. Don't get me started about that pathetic goatee, good grief. Mary Helen talked to me about how she walked by and thought the place was being robbed until she recognized you. Do something about your appearance, Gus. I mean it."

"I'm dressed like everyone else. I don't like to waste time with my hair so I keep it clipped." I ran my hand over the fine buzz on my head.

She ignored my comments, turned abruptly and did a quick tour of the store. She marched back to me.

"You have to grow up one day," she said.

"According to you, I never will. Remember?"

"Not when it comes to women. You'll always screw anything in a skirt. I'm talking about the rest of your life."

I recognized the path we had stumbled onto. Sylvia would bring up my mistakes and I'd get defensive and before either one of us could stop it, we'd be hollering at each other. She might end up crying and I might break something to make a point. Two years and the wounds were still open and painful.

"Please, we don't have to do this," I said. "I messed up. I'm sorry. It's been a long time. Let it go."

She opened her mouth to scream back at me, but stopped before any sound came out. She shook her hair out of her eyes, raised her hand and flipped her wrist in an attempt to wave me out of her life, again.

She dashed through the doorway that led to the back room and the alley door. I heard her open and then slam it shut. There went the bright, pleasant day.

Bob Marley sang about how every little thing was gonna be all right, but I wasn't buying any reggae feel-good right then. Leave it to Sylvia to ruin a great song.

I wanted to blame her for everything, including losing my job and the general disaster known as the U.S. economy.

I examined the photograph again. I convinced myself that the smudge on the girl's shoulder had to be a bruise, not a hickie, tattoo or dirt, and that she had tried to cover it with make-up. Artie could have been the cause of the bruise, and not necessarily because he lost himself in the throes of ecstasy. On the other hand, it could have come from her blackmailing partner when he tried to keep her in line, or from another victim of her scam who lashed out when he heard the price she demanded for her silence.

I put the photograph back in the desk and tried to keep busy.

The Denver Post predicted more showers for that afternoon. I read the forecast at least six times, along with a couple of passes through the adventures of Beetle Bailey, Funky Winkerbean and Doonesbury. An elderly pair of chatty sisters cruised the store, hardly looking at the goods as they dished on several of their neighbors back "at the home." I swept the floor for the third time that week. I checked the dumpster in the alley and made sure no homeless guy had crawled in and died. I plugged in my cell phone and charged the battery. A fire truck roared a couple blocks away through the intersection at Clay and Thirty-Second. I chased a cat from the front door.

I never stopped thinking about Sylvia.

About an hour after Sylvia left, a dark sedan parked in front of the shop. Two men in sport coats and slacks exited the car, removed sunglasses, looked up and down the street and then walked to the store's entrance. The smell of cigarettes followed them into Sylvia's shop.

The older man, about forty-five, white and tired-looking, wore wrinkled pants and apparently was out of shape—red face, labored breathing even though he walked only about fifteen feet. The cigarette smell floated off his tan coat. The second, younger man was African American. His neat pants gave him an all-around smoother edge than his partner. The men looked serious, almost angry. They were obvious police and I worried. No visit from a cop had ever turned out good.

The older man looked down on me as I sat at the table. The younger man stood behind him and off to the side where he had a clear view of me, the back of the store and the front door.

"Gus Corral?" the older one asked.

"Yeah, that's me."

He studied me, looking for a weapon, I guessed. The pair's body language said they were cautious but in command. The older one focused on me while his pal made sure the surroundings were secure.

"I'm detective Reese, Paul Reese. My partner is Frank Robbins." He flashed his badge at me. Robbins didn't bother. "We'd like to talk with you for a few minutes."

I stood up and both Reese and Robbins frowned.

"Sure. What's this about?"

"We're checking a few things and we think you can help us with our investigation."

"Investigation? You think I can help? That'd be a new one, for you and me, wouldn't it?"

"I'm sorry, Mr. Corral. I don't understand," Reese said. "Just a few questions. We're looking into a string of burglaries that may be related. We're talking to a lot of people in the neighborhood, including the businesses. This is the kind of place where some of the stolen stuff could end up." Robbins smiled at that remark.

Reese paused and watched me but when I didn't react, he continued. "Not that you had anything to do with the burglaries, but the thieves might have tried to sell you some of their stolen goods, maybe they tried to get quick cash out of you for the loot?"

I relaxed. I had nothing to fear from a fishing expedition. As far as anyone knew I was clean as mother's milk. The fallout from the divorce forced good behavior on me. Thank you, Sylvia, for that at least.

"You can look, if you think anything's here, if that's what you're saying," I said. "No one's tried to sell me stolen property in a long time. No one's tried to sell me anything in a long time. So I think you picked the wrong segunda to check out."

"Segunda?" Reese asked.

"Second-hand store," Robbins said. "That's what they call these places."

Reese nodded as though he knew who "they" were.

Robbins stepped forward. He unfolded a piece of yellow paper and handed it to me. "Here's a list of the stolen items. Why don't you look it over and see if anything rings a bell? If you remember anyone trying to get rid of this type of merchandise?"

I scanned a two-column list of about fifty things—laptops, quite a bit of computer equipment, flat screens, jewelry, paintings, coats, sweaters and more.

"You can see, we don't have much." I aimed the list at the far wall of the store to emphasize my point. "No TVs, no laptops, except for Sylvia's." I moved to my left to give them a better view of the laptop sitting on the table. "No real jewelry, all the costume junk is in that cabinet over there by the old magazines. No coats or sweaters, but we have plenty of little girls' dresses and baby bibs. Like I said, there hasn't been anyone trying to sell me anything in a long time, a couple of months at least. Two old computer printers against the wall back there." I pointed again. "They've been here at least a year."

Neither of the cops moved. Robbins took back his list, folded it lengthwise and slipped it inside his sports coat.

"You been working here for what, almost two years?" Reese asked.

"Sounds like you know the answer to your question. But what's that got to do with burglaries?"

"Before you started here you were a delivery man for Juanita's Foods. Tortillas, frozen chile sauce, tamale leaves. Did that for three, four years before that place shut down?"

The two cops stood between me and the door.

"What're you getting at? Enlighten me. You sure aren't looking for stolen property."

This time Reese brought out a piece of paper from inside his coat.

"No, Gus. That's wrong. We are dealing with burglaries and stolen goods. Kind of. We're not attached to the Burglary and Theft Unit but it seemed like a good idea to kill two birds in one trip. When your name came up, Frank and I figured it was worth a shot to look into the burglaries, too. Since we were planning to visit you anyway." He unfolded the paper. "Because of this. Now, this is something I'm sure you know about and you can explain it to us. Right, Gus?" He handed the paper to me. A copier image of a check was printed in the center of the page.

Pay to the order of Gus Corral the sum of one thousand dollars and no cents. Signed by Arturo Baca.

My insides knotted and I tasted sour blueberries and bitter coffee.

"Uh, what is this?" The words popped out of my mouth without me thinking about them. I had to cover my ass, play dumb. I couldn't admit anything, not yet, not without knowing what I was getting into. I handed the sheet back to Reese. He re-folded the paper and stuck it in his pocket.

"You saying you don't know why Artie Baca made out a check for a thousand dollars to you? You never saw it before, Gus? That's what you're saying? Your old friend didn't owe you for a favor, never asked you to do something for him? Because it sure looks like you were getting paid by Artie for something. I don't think he was the kind of guy who would give away a thousand bucks."

"No one's given me a thousand dollars, ever. Do I look like someone who gets thousand dollar checks from old friends? What could I do for a guy like Artie Baca?"

"That's a good question, Gus." Robbins piped up this time. "What could a guy like you do for Artie Baca that's worth a thousand dollars?"

Bag man. Errand boy. Target. Artie had wanted me for all three, and I had taken the job with gratitude.

"It's not kosher." Reese tapped a pack of cigarettes against his wrist. "You," he practically spit out the word, "being paid a grand by a player like Artie Baca. The idea offends my common sense. I doubt the money was for any of your junk. The entire place can't be worth a thousand dollars." His pale skin darkened as he spoke. "We got us a real puzzle here, Gus. We need the truth. Now, here, today."

Robbins nodded his head and drifted closer to his partner. His smile had spread across his jaw. The cops moved in for the kill.

My heart pumped anxiety and excitement. My legs went rubbery and my eyes strained for clarity. Again, the kid from the North Side had to stand up to hassle from outsiders—cops, other kids, strangers. I had to de-escalate, be smart.

I spread my fingers and held up my hands at waist level, like I was surrendering. "Whoa, boys. Don't get carried away. Why don't you ask Artie what the check is for? Why do you have it anyway? What . . . "

Reese coughed. A cigarette appeared in his hand. Robbins finally quit smiling. I heard the wall clock tick. The temperature in the room must have risen by ten degrees in the time since the cops arrived. The meaning of the cops' visit flowed over me. I grabbed the back of my chair to stop the flash of dizziness. "That would be hard to do, right, Gus?" Reese said. "Considering we found the check in Artie's wallet when we searched his dead body. Artie can't explain anything, not with a bullet hole where his heart should be. So that leaves you, Gus. I'm all ears." He flicked a lighter and lit his cigarette. Smoke poured from Reese's mouth. He coughed again. Robbins fanned the smoke away from his face.

"Here's an idea, Gus," Robbins said. "The thousand dollars was a payoff. Don't know for what, but my bet would be that it was not on the up-and-up. That's the connection a guy like you might have to Baca." What kind of guy did they think I was? "Maybe you wanted more from Artie, a raise, but he wouldn't pay. Or he thought you did crummy work. Not worth the price you were charging. There's an argument. It gets out of hand. You guys end up in a fight? Baca's been in a few punch-outs over the years, right? I could see Artie pulling a gun. He's got a rep as a hot head, a knee-jerk jerk. It could have been self-defense. Is that what happened, Gus?"

Neither one took their eyes off me. They stared and waited.

4

I didn't see Corrine until she stormed through the front door. Not seeing Corrine is hard to do, given her size. But that morning she snuck up on all of us. It was my day for unexpected visitors. First Sylvia, then the cops, now Corrine.

The door banged open and she strutted in like the queen bee. "Hey, Gus," she shouted. "What's goin' on?" The cops flinched—truth is, I shrunk back a little myself.

Her yellow sweatpants and sweatshirt did what they could to cover most of her bulk. She rolled like a lemon across the floor—a giant lemon with a brown pudgy face and a voice a decibel too high for indoors.

The policemen separated and gave her room. She ended up standing next to me in front of the table. I was so happy to see her I gave her a hug. She stepped away, surprised by my unusual brotherly affection.

"These two policemen have some questions," I said. "Something about Artie Baca and a check. I told them I don't have a clue what they're talking about, but they seem to think I'm involved in whatever happened to Artie."

Her carefully trimmed and shaped eyebrows arched sharply at the two detectives.

"We're talking to Mr. Corral, uh, Miss, uh . . . " Reese stammered.

"Corrine, his sister," as though he should have known that important fact all along. "I don't know you. Been on the force for long?"

"Maybe you don't come in contact with homicide cops that much?" Robbins said. "I'd say that's a good thing, right?"

"The less contact I have with cops, the better all around, you and me. You ever work out of District 1?"

"We'll ask the questions, okay?" Reese said.

Corrine turned away from them. "They asking you about Artie?" I nodded. "Don't say anything." She spoke with the authority of experience. "In case they haven't filled you in, he's dead." She emphasized the word "dead." "I saw it on the morning news. They found his body in one of the new condos he's building over by Saint Patrick's. Somebody shot him. A real mess. You better keep your mouth shut, Gus. I hope you haven't already opened your trap. Be like you to dig yourself into a hole without knowing what's going on."

My older sister always knew what was best for me.

"Hold on a minute." Reese rushed to recover his momentum. "You can't tell your brother not to cooperate. That wouldn't be in his interest, or yours."

Anger slipped into his words. But he couldn't intimidate Corrine. She stood toe-to-toe with cops since before she had a license to drive a car. She believed she had to protect her family and her turf, and he made the mistake of messing with both.

"Unless you got a warrant or you're arresting Gus, he shouldn't even say prayers with you guys." Corrine's voice did not waver. "Anybody knows that. It's like basic survival, one-oh-one."

The cops now stared at Corrine. She stared back.

I knew she wouldn't back off. I'd found myself in the same spot as the cops several times and I'd never worked my way through her attitude.

Reese scratched his head. Robbins stuck his hands in the pockets of his sports coat. He said, "This sucks." His words were meant only for Reese, but we all heard them.

Reese straightened himself to his full six feet plus. "We can take care of this now if Gus will answer a few simple questions." He didn't know any better, so he kept trying to convince her that I needed to do the right thing. "We can do it now, or later at the station. It gets real ugly if we have to go downtown. You don't have anything to hide, right?" Reese's question was directed at me but he looked at Corrine.

"Ask away," I said. "It doesn't matter." I was feeling all chingón with my sister at my side.

"No way," Corrine insisted. She folded her arms in front of her sweatshirt and twisted her body into something like a gangster lean. I liked what she was doing but it made me nervous.

"For once," she said, "think this through. If they want to question you about a murder, you need legal help. I'll call a lawyer. Downtown or here at the shop, either way someone has to represent you. This is serious."

She unfolded her arms and dug around in her sweatpants until she produced a cell phone. She punched buttons, looking for the number of an attorney, I hoped.

"If Gus has nothing to hide he doesn't need a lawyer." Detective Reese flipped through a notebook as though he was going to write notes for his file.

"Yeah, right." Corrine looked up from her phone. "Spoken like a TV cop. How many times have I heard that one? Just understand that my brother isn't talking to you unless he has a lawyer. If that means we need to go to your house, let's get with it."

My sister certainly was brave with my personal freedom.

Reese jammed his notebook back in his pocket. "This doesn't look good for you. You're acting like a guilty man. Your sister's advice is all bad."

I opened my mouth but Corrine stepped in front of me, closer to the cops.

"Funny how a cop thinks that when a citizen exercises his rights he must be guilty of something." She put the phone up to her ear. "Hello, Luis? This is Corrine Corral. Yeah, long time. I'd like to catch up but my brother needs help. Like now. You busy for the next couple of hours?"

It did not surprise me that Corrine could get directly to a lawyer on her first call.

Robbins didn't make a sound but it was obvious he was not happy with the way the situation played out. He looked at his watch and fumbled with something in one of his pockets. Then he grabbed Reese by the coat sleeve. "We don't want to waste our time," he said. "We're not getting anything done here today."

"Yeah, you're right," Reese said.

"Hold on, Luis." She spoke to her cell. "The cops are saying something."

"Don't think for a second that this is over, Gus," Reese said. "We're watching you and your sister, now that she's jumped into this business. You just made number one on our shit list, Gus. You can thank her for that." He pointed his finger at Corrine. The two men walked out of the store.

The room darkened as clouds covered the sun. A gust of wind pushed trash along the street. Tree limbs swayed over the sidewalk. The latest rain rolled in to Wheat Ridge at the western edge of the city and waited.

Reese pulled up the lapels of his coat. Robbins squinted against flying dust. I couldn't hear what they said but Robbins clearly was upset. He waved his arms and shook his head while Reese simply nodded. Eventually they drove away without looking back at us.

I filled a glass with water from the sink in the back room, took a drink and a few deep breaths and then walked back to the front.

"Christ, that could have gone bad, Corrine. You should have checked with me first about what you were gonna do. Why . . . " My voice trailed off when I saw that she was still on the phone.

"It's okay, Luis. I'll get back to you." She shut her phone and punched my upper arm.

"Thanks, I guess." I rubbed the instant charley horse in my triceps. "But I could have answered their questions and ended this. They got nothing on me because I haven't done anything."

"Yeah, and only the guilty go to prison. You know better."

"Now they're coming after me, hard. Thanks."

"No problem." She shook her head.

I couldn't tell if she was pissed at me or the cops. Probably both.

"These cops," she said. "They're not used to a woman who knows her rights and has the sense to stand up to them." Corrine could not resist an opportunity to toot her own horn. "But then, they never met me before."

Ah, my older sister. What a jewel. Several women made an impact on my life. Corrine headed the list. She bailed me out of jams, or forced me into situations where I never belonged—situations that only Corrine could have set up—since we were scruffy kids running wild in the alleys and weedy lots of the North Side. The thing that happened not so long ago with Pancho Villa's skull—now that's a classic piece of Corrine drama.

5

The story is repeated every so often in magazines and the Internet. How someone robbed Pancho Villa's grave in 1926 and snatched his head. Emil Homdahl, a mercenary and pre-CIA spy, what they used to call a soldier of fortune, was usually "credited" with the theft. He was arrested in Mexico but released because of lack of evidence—some say because of political pressure from north of the border. Eventually, the story goes, he sold his trophy to Prescott Bush, grandfather of you-know-who. Bush stashed the skull at a fancy college back East.

That's all bull, of course. Oh yeah, Villa's corpse was minus a skull but Homdahl never had it, the poor sap. Everyone overlooked one detail. There was another guy arrested with Homdahl, a Chicano from Los Angeles by the name of Alberto Corral. He was quickly released, too, and then he disappeared off the historical page, unlike Homdahl, who apparently liked the attention and actually enjoyed his grave-robbing notoriety. The public ignored or forgot about Corral's role in the tale. If he's remembered at all, it's as Homdahl's flunky, the muscle who dug up the grave or broke into the tomb, depending on the version of the story, and who was paid with a few pesos and a bottle of tequila while the gringo made twenty-five grand off old man Bush.

I didn't know why Great-grandpa Alberto ended up with the skull and I didn't care. No one ever told me how he was connected to Homdahl or whatever possessed him to want to steal Pancho's head and I didn't expect to find out. What I did know was that the Corral family took care of the skull for as long as I could remember. I doubted that I would ever forget the image of the skull wrapped in old rags or plastic bags and stored in various containers like hatboxes or cardboard chests. As kids we whispered about the skull when we caught glimpses of the creepy yellowish thing whenever the adults dragged it out, usually on the nights when the tequila and beer and whiskey flowed long and strong.

My grandmother Otilia sang to it, the "Corrido de Pancho Villa," of course. The tiny old woman, hunched under a shawl and often with a bandana wrapped around her gray fine hair, drank slowly from a glass of whiskey while she stared at the box that held Panchito—that's what she called it—for several minutes, and meanwhile all the kids waited for what we knew was coming. Without warning, Otilia ripped off the box top, grabbed the skull, exposed it to the light and burst into weepy lyrics about the Robin Hood of Mexico. One of my uncles, also into his cups, would join in with loud strumming on an old guitar. Shouts and whoops and ay-yay-yays erupted from whoever else was in the house, making the little kids scatter from the room, shrieking and crying, while us older ones were hypnotized by the dark eye sockets and crooked teeth of the skull of Pancho Villa.

You can imagine what a jolt it was when the skull was stolen from my sister's house.

I knew Corrine shouldn't have had the skull, but she was the oldest. She claimed rights to the skull and took it out of our parents' house before Maxine, my younger sister, or I knew what was happening. Corrine always said she hated that "disgusting cosa." But there she was, all over Panchito like he was gold. I kind of understood. Panchito was one of the few things our parents left us. The only connection we had to the old-timers of the family.

I argued with Corrine about Panchito. I pointed out that the parade of losers that camped out at her house was a major security risk. I added that I could keep the skull at Sylvia's shop. It fit in with the assorted debris Sylvia liked to stock, but Corrine clutched that skull like a baby and it was clear that the only way I would get my hands on it was to rip it from hers, which I wasn't going to even attempt.

The other thing in Corrine's favor was that she owned a house and lived a fairly respectable life, considering her history and friends. She hired on at the Department of Social Services right out of high school as an office aide and worked herself up through the bureaucracy. When her twenty years were up she got a nice retirement package while she was young enough to enjoy it. Corrine received checks every month from various sources—exes, dividends and other places that were a mystery to me. She had it figured out.

Corrine called me one night around midnight. Not all that unusual, for Corrine. One crisis after another. One of her boys— they all had brats of their own but Corrine still called them her boys—needed to get bailed. Did I have about five hundred dollars? Or she slipped and banged up her knee and couldn't walk or drive. Would I pick her up for bingo? Or the latest love of her sad life went out for a six-pack about a week ago. Could I go look for him?

Corrine's call woke me from a bad dream about a job where I had to kill all the flies, gnats and mosquitoes I chased from a dirty swimming pool. Sylvia was my boss. I crawled off my cot and answered the shop's phone.

"You got your nerve, Gus," Corrine shouted over the line. "I can't believe you took it. What'd you do, pawn it for beer money?"

"What the hell are you screaming about? It's midnight, in case you didn't know."

"Panchito! Panchito!"

As if that explained everything.

A half hour later I had the story and she started to consider that I hadn't broken into her house and stolen the skull. She'd come home from an evening with the girls and found the back door wide open and a pair of her panties on the lawn. She freaked immediately and called the cops. She waited outside, not chancing that the intruder might still be inside. When the cops gave her the all-clear she entered a house torn upside down and inside out. She found her clothes scattered everywhere, drawers ripped from dressers, bowls of food splattered on the kitchen floor and a trail of CD cases snaked from her CD player to the useless back door. The final straw made her hysterical. A large piss puddle stained the middle of her carpet.

Did she think I was really capable of that? I could see how she might be suspicious of me concerning the skull, but to trash her place and pee on her rug? Please.

The cops said they couldn't find any evidence of a forced entry. They concluded that Corrine had left the back door open and one of the neighborhood kids probably had seen it from the alley. A crime of opportunity, they told her. I can picture her face when she heard that. She must have screamed that she was absolutely sure she'd locked the door and then most likely turned into a blubbery mess, but she was just covering. My tough, street-wise sister could also occasionally act scatter-brained.

One time she came home and found a pot of beans completely black, the beans nothing more than a congealed mass. Smoke as thick as her chubby arms filled every room. A fire truck roared up a few minutes later. The drapes and walls smelled like burnt beans for months. She told me she couldn't remember doing anything with beans, much less leaving the stove on.

I agreed with the cops' take on the break-in. The way Corrine's house was messed up and the stuff that was taken—CDs, video tapes, a jar full of pennies and a bag of potato chips—sounded like a kid's thing. But what the hell would he do with a skull?

Corrine never mentioned Panchito to the cops. She told me she had it in a Styrofoam cooler at the back of her coat closet near the front door. The cooler sat in the closet, empty. She guessed the thief took the skull in one of the pillowcases missing from her bed. The cops said that was a tried-and-true method for burglars to haul away their booty, in the vic's own pillowcases or trash bags.

The cops would never arrest anyone. We had so many unsolved break-ins on the North Side that the police gave victims a number to use when they called in to ask about their cases—no name or address, just the number.

The next day I closed the shop early to start asking around but I couldn't say too much. The Corral family hadn't been up front about Panchito. We assumed possession of Pancho's skull was illegal and the desecration of the grave of a Mexican hero certainly wouldn't do anything for the family reputation. Mexico could demand the return of Panchito's head and the U.S. government could back away from us and might declare that we were as illegal as the skull and deport us.

For two days I looked for kids trying to get rid of CDs that didn't seem right for them—Tony Bennett, Frank Sinatra, Miguel Aceves Mejía—and a jar of pennies.

I asked old friends who still called me bro'. I quizzed waitresses at a couple of Mexican restaurants. My questions made more than one pool player nervous. The ballers that crowded the court at Chaffee Park swore they didn't know nada. Those NBA wannabes wouldn't tell me anything anyway.

On the second day my search took me to the beer joints.

I got nothing from the barflies, naturally. They scowled as if I'd asked for money, never a popular question in any bar I'd ever been in. A couple of the souses didn't even look at me when I spoke to them. I decided to take a break. Detective work made me thirsty and the Holiday Bar and Grill served cold beer, but there wasn't a grill in sight.

Accordion music played in the background and a pair of muscular women wearing their boyfriends' colors played eight ball along a side wall. Counting me, three customers at the bar were entertained by Jackie, the bartender who worked the day shift at the Holiday.

Jackie methodically wiped a glass with a bright yellow bar rag and blinked her inch-long eyelashes at me. I worried for a hot sec that the weight of what looked like caterpillars sitting on her eyelids might permanently shut Jackie O's eyes, but it didn't seem to be a problem. Jackie O—that's what she wanted to be called, but I remembered when she was just plain old Javier Ortega, which is another story entirely. I hardly ever used the O in her name. I couldn't bring myself to say it. I had to comment about her outfit and headdress.

"Trying for the Carmen Miranda look today, Jackie?"

"Don't be foolish. These are just a few old things I had around the house. A summer adventure. You like?" She twirled and clapped her hands, kind of in flamenco style. The two guys down the bar coughed up their beer. I kept a straight face.

"Nice. That shade is good on you."

"What you been up to, Gus? I don't see you in here too much anymore."

"Same old, you know how it is." She nodded. "But Corrine got ripped off the other night, maybe you heard about it? They broke in her house and took a couple thousand dollars worth of stuff. At least that's what she told the insurance. Too much, huh? I'm trying to find out who would do such a thing, maybe get some of Corrine's junk back. Maybe kick some ass." I threw that last part in but I knew she knew it was just talk.

She almost dropped the glass. She turned away quickly and helped the two guys who couldn't seem to get enough of her show. I picked up a bad vibe off Jackie and it bothered me. We went back a long ways and I recognized her signals. I sipped on my beer and out of the corner of my eye I could see her looking at me through her heavily accessorized lashes. Again, I felt foolish. This was not like Jackie.

She reached under the bar and grabbed a bottle of what I was drinking. She opened it and brought it to me although I hadn't ordered another.

"Let's have a smoke, Gus. I need one bad."

Now we had moved into strange. For one thing, Jackie knew I didn't smoke. For another, although the anti-smoking ordinance meant that all smoking had to be done outside the premises, I couldn't remember when that particular law had ever been enforced in the Holiday, especially during the day shift when there wasn't anyone in the bar, to speak of.

But I went with it. She snapped her fingers at the women playing pool. "I'll be right back, Lori. Come get me if anyone comes in."

One of the women shouted back, "Whatever."

I followed Jackie's sashaying hips into the alley.

She lit a smoke and dragged on it, all nervous. I waited. Like most of the women in my life—Sylvia, the prime example—Jackie loved drama. Jackie could emote, that's for sure.

When she finished sucking the life out of half the smoke, she whispered, "I shouldn't say anything. But we been friends forever, Gus. You backed me up when I needed it. You can't ever let on that you got this from me. I'll call you a damn liar. I mean it, Gus. You swear, on your mother's grave, Gus? On your mother's grave."

Her face disappeared in the twilight and the glowing tip of her cigarette didn't give off enough light for me to see how serious she was, so I took her at her word.

"Okay, Jackie. I swear. I never heard nothing from you. Which so far is the truth."

"Jessie Salazar was in last night."

I heard that name and I wanted a cigarette.

"I thought he was in the pen," I said. "Limon or Cañon City. Supermax."

"He did five years. Doesn't seem that long, does it? He came in last night. I had to fill in for Ritchie, he got sick or something or I wouldn't even know Salazar was around. He showed up with his old crew. Dressed in a suit, smelling like Macy's perfume counter. Talking loud and mean. Same old crazy Jessie. He said things about your family, and you. That chicken-shit stuff between the Corrals and the Salazars. He said the great payback had begun, that's what he called it, but that there was more hell to pay. He talks like that, remember?"

I felt like someone had punched my gut.

"He never got over that Corrine testified against him," Jackie said. "I didn't think anything about it last night. That happens in here all the time. Guys blow off steam then the next day forget all about it. More so if the guy just got out of the joint. But when you said someone broke into Corrine's house, I put two and two together. Salazar's that kind of punk. He could have trashed Corrine's house, easy, but if he did, that's just the beginning. You got to tell her, and you watch your back, Gus. He always thought you should have stopped her, controlled Corrine. He blames you for him doing time."

Jackie stomped on her cigarette. "I better get back to work. Cuídate, Gus. Be careful."

I gave her a weak smile and walked away through the alley. I stopped and turned and waved at Jackie. "Thanks," I said. She blew a kiss at me.

Crazy Jessie had been my number one problem for most of my life. He played the role of school bully and then the neighborhood gangster. Eventually he passed through reform school and the state penitentiary. I tangled with him several times when we were younger. My mother and his mother were rivals when they were low-riding North Side cholas, and I'd heard many stories about parties gone bad, fights on school yards and in nightclubs. That nonsense just kept on when they had their own kids. Corrine and I often brushed up against Jessie and his brothers and sisters, not always coming out on top. But we held our own.

About six years ago Corrine was having dinner with her latest honey when Jessie stormed into La Cocina restaurant waving a handgun. He terrorized the customers, pistol-whipped the owner and took cash, wallets, purses and jewelry. Jessie was strung out bad on his drug of choice. Corrine talked to the cops and identified Jessie without hesitation, but her date denied recognizing the gunman. Hell, he wasn't sure that there had even been a disturbance. Didn't matter to Corrine. She didn't see it as snitching. She had to protect her family and her turf even if that meant speaking up in court and pointing her finger at Jessie.

I was proud of her but also a little bit nervous. We all relaxed when they turned Jessie over to the Department of Corrections. We thought he would be gone for a very long time. Five years didn't seem long enough, but then I never understood the so-called justice system.

I knew where to find Jessie. But I didn't know if I wanted to find him. I had to warn Corrine, and I gave serious consideration to forgetting about Panchito. The thug might have left us alone after he vented on Corrine's property and he found the skull. I could see him shaking his head about his discovery in Corrine's closet, thinking that the Corrals were way weirder than he'd always assumed.

I called Corrine but the service was weak. I got a busy signal, but that wasn't right. I should have connected to her voice mail. I debated where to go—Corrine's or Jessie's.

To get to Jessie's crib I had to drive in the opposite direction from Corrine. His small house overlooked the interstate from a hill where several new condos were going up. Yuppie hell, Sylvia called it. The house had been the Salazar home forever and it always had been a dump. With the wave of newcomers and the construction frenzy, the shack must have doubled or tripled in value since Jessie did his time, although Jessie would never know what to do with that piece of information. One of his deadbeat sisters technically owned the place, but as sure as I knew that Jessie's urine stained my sister's carpet, I also knew he lived in that house.

I could have turned it over to the police. That didn't happen in my world. Where I came from, the cops weren't the first line of defense. I grew up constantly squaring off against cabrones like Jessie. Every lousy week another clown would challenge my manhood and I would have to beat or get beaten. The cops did not help. Back then, I did not want to explain to my old man why my sister came home in tears and I didn't do a damn thing about the bastard who slapped her around. The payback was my responsibility. I learned early about waking up in a cell in the City Jail, staring down the ugly face of what my life could become if I didn't do the right thing. Not the cops, teachers or friends. Me. I had to do the right thing.

I stopped for gas and used the restroom at the 7-Eleven. Stalling, for sure. Driving to Jessie's took a while but eventually I got there.

I parked about a block away and did my best to look inconspicuous. A few of the projects had crews working late, overtime. Steel beams stretched to the sky and white concrete slabs waited. Trucks, earth movers and bull dozers parked everywhere. I played ball in these lots when I was a kid, made out with girls and drank beer and shake-em-up with my pals. When I was alone I fantasized about Isabel Scutti. No one who ever lived in the new buildings would know that or care about those things. I hardly cared myself.

I made my way up the alley behind Jessie's house. I picked up a piece of rebar, two feet long, not thinking about how inadequate it was for the job I had to do. The night had a gray tint from the construction lights. Hip-hop blasted from Jessie's back yard. I crawled behind a dumpster and peeked through the chain-link fence.

Jessie sprawled on the dirt. An ugly hole in his head leaked blood and a messy soup of other stuff. I admit I was relieved.

The guy standing over the body, holding a gun, looked like a junior version of Jessie, except he was alive. Another worthless gangbanger, extracting his own revenge for whatever Jessie might have inflicted, maybe in that back yard that evening, maybe in a jail cell that was too small for the both of them, maybe years ago for something that Jessie couldn't remember.

I guessed no one heard the shot. The construction noise could have drowned it out or the rap music might have covered up the crime. Sometimes gunshots have no sound on the North Side.

The guy spit on Jessie. A strange thought came to me. "DNA, dummy." He tucked the gun in the back waist of his pants and jumped over the fence. I inched closer to the dumpster and my luck held. He walked the other way, whistling.

I swung open the gate and tried to sneak into the back yard. I acted because I had to. Corrine and Panchito were counting on me. For a sec I held back. I didn't want to end up like Jessie. I shook off my hesitation and moved. I did what I had to do, like always. No one else was in the house. I realized that whoever had capped Jessie would have made sure of that. I looked all over that yard, except at the oozing body at my feet.

Panchito perched on a concrete block. A lime green sombrero with red dingle balls balanced on his slick shiny head and a droopy cigar dangled from his mouth hole. I was embarrassed for him. I removed the hat and cigar and picked him up. A dirty pillowcase spread out on the ground. I wrapped Panchito in it.

It was a long walk back to my car and a long drive to Corrine's. I never heard any sirens, and no one stopped me. I drove in silence thinking about what had happened, trying to piece together coincidence and luck. I never thought so hard in my life. My luck had been amazing and I toyed with the idea of going back to the 7-Eleven for a lottery ticket. But I wasn't the lucky type. Never won anything in my life. I thought even harder about what had happened.

Corrine slowly opened the door. She let me in but didn't say anything. I set the bundle on her kitchen table.

She smiled.

"How'd you find out about Jessie? Who was that guy?" I blurted my questions as quickly as I could. I didn't want to give her time to make up something.

"You're the smart one. Figure it out yourself."

"Jackie. She called you, told you what she told me. Said I was probably going over to Jessie's."

"Close. She said you were on your way to get killed by that son-of-a-bitch."

"The shooter? What's his story?"

"You remember him. Charley Maestas. He lived here about six months, a while back. Too young for me, turned out. He owed Jessie for a lot of grief, something awful about his sister, but he had to wait for Jessie to do his time. I let Charley know that Jessie was out and where he could find him and the rest was up to him. I might have said that Jessie was getting ready to book, so he had to deal with him tonight. I thought the least Charley could do was give you some help if you got over your head. I guess Charley took care of the whole thing?" She asked but she didn't really want an answer. "Only the strong survive," she said.

I shrugged. It turned out to be simple. Corrine and one of the men in her sad love life. North Side justice often was simple. Direct, bloody and simple.

My older sister picked up Panchito and gave him a quick wipe with the pillowcase. She carried him to the closet, dug out the cooler, placed the skull in it and shut the door.

I walked out the back and I hollered, "I like the new rug."

6

"**I**s this something stupid again?" Corrine said.

I hated when she used that word around me. "Don't call me stupid. In fact, you can go to hell."

Her eyes squeezed together. "Easy, little brother. If the cops are jammin' you, you need my help. It's always been that way."

Obviously, but I didn't have it in me to admit it. "I can deal with it. Like you say, only the strong survive."

"And that's you? A person needs smarts, too. Be strong, and smart."

I should have given in. I didn't. "I can deal with this."

"Okay, Gus. Let's start over. How about lunch? I didn't have breakfast. I'll eat and you tell me what the hell you got yourself into this time."

"Sure, we can talk. Just don't get all up on me. I don't want the hassle."

We decided to eat at Chencha's Taquería, about a block away. We agreed that we had enough time before the weather hit, at least until we made it to the restaurant. Gusts of wind sporadically twirled paper, leaves and cigarette butts around us as we walked. The western sky turned to gun barrel gray but the rain hadn't made it to the North Side yet. I smelled the rain coming and made the mistake of telling Corrine.

"Rain doesn't have a smell," she said. "That's an old wives' tale."

"I'm smelling something, and it's the same thing I smell every time before it rains. How do you explain that?"

"Do I look like a weatherman?"

"Then how do you know that rain doesn't have a smell?"

"Because I don't smell anything except the garbage in that trash can, the dog shit on the curb and your B.O."

I let her jabber on with only a few grunts from me. We stopped at the taquería and sat at one of the rickety tables, ordered our food and tried to act like a regular brother and sister.

Chencha had redecorated. Several framed black and white photographs of early Denver hung on each wall. The same mass-produced pictures greeted tourists in downtown bars and restaurants. I hadn't expected them in an old North Side favorite. The poster-sized photos showed scenes from the city's history that recalled Wild West legends and boom town excitement: a trolley rolling down Larimer Street, a well-dressed crowd under the arch at Union Station, a horse dragging a wagon in snow in front of the Capitol. I would not have been surprised to see portraits of Butch Cassidy and the Sundance Kid, or H.A.W. Tabor and his main squeeze Baby Doe. No photographs of Mexicans. Guess we weren't around when the photographer set up his equipment. We were probably picking crops for shipping on the next train, or lugging silver from Tabor's mines, or standing lookout at the Hole-in-the-Wall hideout.

"What are you smiling about?" Corrine said.

"Nothing. Just enjoying the company. I got hungry."

"You're a strange one, brother. I ever tell you that?"

Corrine and Maxine were my best friends but they didn't know me. They thought they had me figured out, but how could they? The puzzle of Gus Corral was all illusion—disappearing fog on a cracked mirror. My sisters looked for answers about their brother that didn't exist.

I had disappointed them for years. They often told me how they expected a lot from me because of my grades in school and my arrogant talk about what I wanted to do with my life. In my teen years I played with the idea of an engineer or scientist. I could handle math, numbers made sense. Their logic came easy. But the dreams and ambitions from several lifetimes ago never panned out. The years after high school slipped by almost unnoticed by me. I lacked whatever made others succeed. I couldn't find the secret that would move me to the next level. I failed at work, my marriage, and in my own head. Strange as it sounds, I sometimes blamed Artie Baca for my failures.

On the other hand, my sisters jumped all over life and, each in their own style, beat it into submission. Corrine didn't let anything get in the way of her having what she wanted, including men. She poured her heart's blood into neighborhood projects, volunteer work and having a good time. Flamboyant, that was Corrine.

Max tried to fly under the radar. She couldn't pull that off. She wanted to lose herself in the crowd, but that would never happen. Despite her built-in reluctance, she succeeded in whatever she tried, from computer tech to managing a head banger band. She enjoyed the company of several boyfriends and girlfriends. Max had "popularity" written all over her lifestyle, which remained a mystery to me and something I'd never dug into too deeply. Not because I didn't care. Her world blurred gender lines, reversed accepted roles and shattered expectations, but those things were irrelevant to me as long as Max was happy.

When Corrine and I had taken a few bites out of our tacos—pollo and carnitas for me, asada and hamburger for Corrine—she started with her questions.

"What do you know about Artie getting shot? What are you even doing with a guy like Baca?"

I kept eating. One thing about Chencha Hernández is that she makes the kind of salsa that will cauterize your tongue but you can't stop eating it until you are about to pass out. I chugged Chencha's strong iced tea. It didn't help.

"Well, Gus? What did those cops want with you?"

I couldn't ignore her, seeing as how she was about six inches from my face. I put down the tea and dug out the photograph. I handed it to Corrine.

"My, how decadent. So bourgeois." Corrine could talk like that without being aware of how phony she sounded. "Artie give you this? Who's the girl? The cops ask you about her?"

"No, no. They don't know about her. At least they don't know about this picture. I got it from Artie. He came by the other day, talking about his trouble with the young lady."

"Don't tell me. She's knocked up and wanted Artie to pay for the kid."

"That's what I thought, too. But, no, that ain't it. She just wanted money, period. Seems there's a video that exposes much more of Artie."

"Blackmail? Really? You don't hear that one much anymore."

She chomped into her taco and chewed. The salsa did its job and she reached for her glass of water. Her eyes welled up. After she swallowed, she said, "If the cops don't know about this picture and the girl, then what were they talking to you about?"

"They found a check on Artie's body, made out to me. For a thousand dollars."

She dropped her fork.

I explained Artie's visit and the job he wanted me to do. I emphasized the thousand dollars. I went over how Artie and I sketched out the drop, and I made sure she knew my reservations about the plan. In fact, I had decided not to do it. I added that Artie hadn't talked with me since his visit.

"Which seems understandable now," I said.

"Oh, little brother. You just don't learn, do you? You trust anybody. Sorry lover-boy Baca was setting you up for something. You don't know the whole story. You don't really know what went down between him and the girl."

"I don't care about that. It was a chance for a job."

She put her elbows on the table and leaned into her clenched hands. "She must be working with someone. She needs back up."

"Artie didn't mention anyone else."

"Well, it looks like Artie met the guy. Which didn't turn out too good for him."

She ate another bite of food and swallowed another long drink of water. "Asking for ten thousand," she said. "The girl must have something big on Artie, something he didn't tell you. That something might have cost him his life. But you, good old Gus Corral, Mr. Nice Guy, you're willing to get involved. Why is that?"

"For a thousand bucks, Corrine. I need the money."

She bugged me, dug deep under my skin, and the last time she did that I told myself I wouldn't let it happen again. Fat chance.

"We all need money, Gus. That doesn't mean we all get to act stupid."

I loved my sister. I liked Maxine better, but I loved them both. What Corrine told me wasn't new. I'd heard the same song from her since I was at least fourteen, the first time I faced serious trouble. But still, she could get to me. Maybe it was the shock of Artie's death or the surprise visit from Reese and Robbins. Whatever, that day, she got to me.

"Screw this." I threw my taco on my plate and stood up. "I'm out of here. Enjoy the rest of your lunch by yourself. I told you not to call me stupid." I tossed a ten-dollar bill on the table.

"Sit down, Gus. Don't get mad. Where you off to? It's gonna rain."

I bolted for the door. I heard her laughing behind my back. She never took me seriously.

I regretted my snit-fit almost immediately. I needed Corrine, if only for somebody to talk with, to think things through.

I had to run the last hundred yards to the shop. A hard shower erupted over Highlands and caught me on the street. Rain pelted me as I jumped overflowing curbs. The temperature dropped and the water soaked lawns and flower gardens. My near-bald head dripped rain into my eyes. I stopped under a storefront canopy and waited out the cloudburst.

The reality of the situation took hold. Artie Baca was dead, murdered. The cops knew I had a connection to him and that I had played hard-to-get. They'd be back and they wouldn't be as easy to shake, especially if Corrine wasn't around.

But my stomach didn't rumble because of Reese and Robbins, or because of Chencha's authentic chile. I could explain the check. I had the photo and the girl could be tracked down. She might deny the blackmail attempt but if she was as weak as Artie said, the cops could figure out her scam. I might look like a sucker for get-ting involved—what else was new—and I might get heat about not reporting the blackmail to the police, but at least it'd be clear that I had no reason to kill Artie. Maybe that was wishful thinking. They had me in their sights, so why look for anyone else?

The bullet hole in Artie's heart, as Reese colorfully put it, had me looking over my shoulder at tree-lined Thirty-Second Avenue. Was my loose connection to Artie and Misti Ortiz enough to make me a target, too? The cops were on me already so it wouldn't be much longer until Misti and her partner-in-shakedowns also stopped by for a chat. Once I started down paranoia road, my imagination took me to extremes of conspiracies and plots and ugly endings. I owed it to myself to know more about the girl, to learn answers to the questions Corrine asked. Knowledge is power and right then I felt like the ninety-seven-pound weakling who had sand kicked in his face.

The rain slowed down and then quit. Large drops of water fell from the trees and the corner drains bubbled and churned from the sudden flow. Thunder continued to boom in the background and lightning creased the southern sky. As always, it took only a few minutes for the air to suck up the moisture and the tempera-ture to climb back up, for life to resume from the wet interruption. The rain smell drifted strong and complete.

In the aftermath of the quick storm, Thirty-Second again buzzed with people, dogs, scooters and cars. A half-dozen kids jammed the counter of the ice-cream shop a block from Sylvia's place. Three bicyclists, decked out in racing colors and profession-al helmets, stood near their wet bikes on the corner of Thirty-Second and Zuni. They stared at a map. Across the street, a Chicano with a soul patch waited by the door to the liquor store. A family that looked like tourists exited the pizza joint, opened umbrellas and crossed the intersection. I assumed they wanted to avoid the dude waiting for his six-pack. They hesitated when they realized they had to walk past me.

Noise and motion took over a street where I once ran, jumped and shouted unnoticed, where I lost myself in stories of what my life might become. Everything had changed, and yet nothing had changed. Off to the east, Denver's downtown skyline simultaneously reflected sunshine and tumbling dark clouds. Glass and steel towered over the orchestrated chaos of a big city. Old warehouse districts and venerable neighborhoods circled the metro core. I heard the city's beat and recognized the rhythm. That view and tempo always provided the background for everything important that happened to me. They gave me a comfort I couldn't explain. They cleared my head so I could think.

By the time I unlocked the door to the shop I convinced myself to help the cops, in my own way. Give them somebody else to think about for Artie Baca's killing. Point them in the direction of the most likely suspects: Misti Ortiz and her unknown associate. I walked into a muggy store and left the door open. I found a towel and dried my head and my arms.

I didn't know exactly how I would carry out my plan, but I knew how to begin. I needed to talk with Misti Ortiz.

7

It should be easy to find an attractive young Latina with a pierced eyebrow who indulged in blackmail. It should.

I knew a guy. Jerome Rodríguez. Down and dirty, a loco from way back who traveled the low road but survived.

Jerome had been through it all—combat, divorce, prison, homelessness, money. I knew my fair share of guys like that. More than once he mentioned his surprise at reaching his fortieth birthday.

That milestone caused Jerome to step back and look at his life. His decision to take on an honest business looked like it came out of nowhere, but he planned it in detail. He opened a coffee shop close enough to the gentrified condos to attract the young professionals but far enough from the trendy retail blocks to keep his rent manageable. His customers were "the hustlers," he said, and he meant that in a good way. When I asked about his business plan, he said, "Hustlers and coffee go together like rice and beans." He named his shop Jerry's Cup O'Joe, but only people who didn't know him called him Jerry.

Jerome simmered with advice and ideas, especially about making money. Some made sense, some were silly and many were illegal. I hadn't gone along with any of his crazier ideas but I had to admit that he tempted me. When the recession hit like a Manny Pacquiáo combination and I lost my job, then my marriage and finally my self-respect, I seriously considered his offer to relieve a neighboring state's bank of some of its bags of cash that, according to Jerome, were "sitting around waiting to be plucked, like college girls at their first frat party." I didn't go through with it, but Jerome knew he almost had me. I'm sure he filed that away for future reference.

Jerome was the guy to see for leads on a woman like Misti Ortiz. I met him at Jerry's the morning after Reese and Robbins introduced themselves to me. He wore a snow white Panama with a rainbow-colored band, and a florid shirt, not quite Hawaiian but close. He nodded at me when I walked in, but he was busy greeting customers and barking orders to the pair of young baristas who jumped at his every word. I ordered, picked up my drink, found an empty chair on the patio and sat down, read the newspaper. Patios and outdoor eating and drinking were big in the neighborhood that summer.

Jerome and I first hooked up back when the tables were turned. I had money and he was down and out. One Saturday afternoon I filled in for Sylvia at her shop, this was long before our divorce. He lugged in a box of old 45s and asked, "How much for the lot?" No small talk, no attempt to grease his sales pitch. All business—typical Jerome.

I rifled through the vinyl and couldn't believe the music that the bearded stranger who needed a haircut brought into the store. The collection had hits from the fifties and sixties, real classics for which any lowriding vato loco would gladly trade a tattoo or two. The Miracles, Four Tops, Jerry Butler, El Chicano, Tierra and other songs and groups that every oldies collector considered basics. But his box also held songs that had to be difficult to find in their original version—"Hey Señorita" by the Penguins, "It's Got to be Mellow" by Leon Haywood, "I Guess That Don't Make Me a Loser" by the Brothers of Soul. Too much Motown, a bit of Philly Soul and plenty of the East Los Angeles sound. Then I got excited. The prizes were a couple of red Elvis Presley discs with original sleeve covers: "That's All Right" and "Good Rockin' Tonight."

I could have offered Jerome ten bucks for everything and he would have been satisfied. But I didn't do it. I bought the box of 45s for twenty-five dollars, minus the Presley records. I gave him the name and number of a local collector who would give him book price for Elvis and I sent him on his way. He looked surprised but he took the money and rushed out of the store.

I listened to the records until the ancient phonograph I borrowed from Sylvia broke down. A few weeks passed and I couldn't find the box of records. She told me she sold it to a neighbor for decorations for his daughter's sweet sixteen "sock-hop" party. He thought it would be a kick to use the 45s as wall hangings and drink coasters. The neighbor ended up with his decorations and Sylvia pocketed twenty dollars. Zilch for yours truly.

Jerome called me his friend after that, and I liked to hang out with him to listen to his stories, ideas and general bullshit. He bounced back months later, bought some decent clothes. Eventually, I found a flyer announcing his new enterprise taped to the shop's front door. I never learned all the details of how he turned his life around. Sometimes we joked about the old records and what happened to them. He didn't tell me how much he pocketed for the Presley songs, but he made at least enough for a shave and a haircut.

Jerome finally joined me on his patio.

"I only have a few minutes, Gus. What's up?"

"You okay? The stress is starting to show. Maybe time for some R and R?"

"God, don't get me started. I ain't got time for no vacation. Can't even hardly take a leak without something going wrong somewhere."

"How come your business is rolling along when everybody else needs a bailout?"

"Those scurvy dogs, so-called financial experts, can kiss my ass. Them and the crooked banks, and this guy Obama and his stooges. All of them together, against the little guy, the small businessman."

"I didn't know you were so political, and a Republican too."

That made him laugh. "I sound like one, don't I? Me and Sarah Palin. Could get real interesting."

"Seriously, dude. How's business?"

"I thought we would go under, drown in the toilet they call the economy, just like everybody else, but lately we're doing all right. Timing is everything. When we opened there weren't that many coffee places around here. That's changing, but we can handle the competition. I have to admit I'm surprised. It's been up and down, and my bottom line changes month to month. Some nights I can't sleep. My hair is falling out. I wonder if it's worth it."

"You should have jumped on the medical marijuana bandwagon," I said. "Those places are popping up everywhere. Thirty-Eighth Avenue has at least one every block. They make serious money, from what I read. No recession in the kush trade."

He nodded. "Yeah, I gave that business some thought, but with my record no way a drug store could be in my name. My moral character is suspect, if you can believe that. But you're right. Those shops are raking it in. Years ago, who'd a thought that the grass business would go legit and your average dope dealer could make beaucoup bucks. We all knew weed was good for chillin'. I might need a prescription myself. I'm kind of tense lately."

His face opened up into a broad, shiny smile that matched his hat.

He had a steady flow of customers ordering coffee, tea or juice, often with pastries or breakfast burritos. Several tables were occupied by chatty young mothers surrounded by baby strollers. A pair of dogs paced near the entrance, occasionally growling at passing joggers.

I sipped on my cappuccino—hot, creamy, eye-opening. I'm an instant coffee guy most of the time, but Jerome had a way with steamed milk and very dark coffee beans that was hard to resist, especially at seven-thirty in the morning. He claimed he learned about coffee while on military duty in the Middle East, but when I asked him for details he changed the subject. That was Jerome—full of stories but only up to a point.

We small-talked for a few minutes more but Jerome didn't contribute much to the conversation. He shook his crossed legs and tapped his fingers on the table top.

"You anxious to get back to work?" I said.

"I'm busy, man. It's not good for the staff to see me sitting around when I should be helping out. Being the boss ain't all that it's made out to be, certain obligations and responsibilities, know what I mean?"

"We could have met at your house, later. This was your choice."

"Only because you sounded desperate. Like a man on fire. What the hell's going on with you now?"

I fished Misti's photograph from my T-shirt pocket and handed it to Jerome. His eyes blinked and his lungs sucked in a quick deep breath of air. The bright smile disappeared.

"You know her?" I said.

He did a classic look-around his shop and nodded. "What you doing with this? Why do you have a picture of Misti Ortiz?"

"It's a long story. When we have more time I'll give you all the details. For now, I need to talk with her. Can you put me in touch?"

He handed back the photo and shook his head. "Trust me. You don't want to touch that, in any way. She's nothing but trouble, Gus. Way over your head. In fact, I don't want to know any more about this photo or the guy with her or why you have it. Just back off. Back off."

"I told you, I need to talk to her. Seriously. It's important. Like life or death."

"Important enough to get you hurt, maybe killed?" He pointed at the photograph in my hand. "That is one dangerous young lady."

"Look, Jerome. No need to get complicated. I just want an address or a phone number. I'll do the rest. Either you have the digits or you don't. It's that simple. Anyway, I heard she wasn't all that tough, or bad. Kind of weak, actually, weepy."

Jerome laughed at the word "weepy." "Whoever told you that is as wrong as tamales in a can. She moves with a heavy crowd, Gus. Nothing like you're used to. Not the bangers we have around here. Those guys are juvenile delinquents compared to Ortiz's people."

I had a hard time thinking of Jessie Salazar and Charley Maestas as "delinquents."

"All right, Jerome. You don't want to tell me anything about this person. Fine. I'll ask somebody else. If she's all you say, someone knows how I can find her. I thought because we go back a ways, and all. But, okay, don't worry about it."

"I'm trying to help you, Gus. I'm saying to stay away from that girl."

Jerome did not exaggerate or play a role. He told it the way he saw it. I trusted his instincts. His warning had me concerned. I shrugged off the feeling and finished the cappuccino. His attention shifted to the line of customers that now wormed outside the door.

"Gus, I have to get back to work."

"Okay. I'll tell Ms. Ortiz you said hi when I find her."

He shook his head. "Christ. If you're going to keep after her, let me check on a few things. I'll make some calls. Maybe I can keep you from getting your hard head shot off. Soon as I have verification from a couple of people, I'll hit you back. You at the same cell number?"

"Yeah, the same." I reached across the table and we bumped knuckles. "Thanks, Jerome."

"Don't thank me. After you see what you're into, let me know then if you're still grateful. 'Gracias' might not be the word that comes to mind."

If Jerome said something or someone meant trouble, I could take that to the bank. For a second I thought about telling him to forget about it. I'd accept his advice and stay away from Misti Ortiz and her hoodlum friends. I'd go back to wasting time at Sylvia's store, running errands for my wacky sister Corrine and trying to stay ahead of bill collectors and repo men. Why stick my finger into a mess created by Artie Baca? I had enough problems already, didn't I?

But I couldn't forget that Artie was dead. Cops were digging into my life. I was trying to protect myself from the same ending as Artie or an arrest by the cops. Anyway, what else did I have to do other than a boring day job and boring nights watching TV in the back of Sylvia's shop?

Knowledge is power—I repeated to myself. The echo came back—*ignorance is bliss.*

8

After my conversation with Jerome I used the shop's computer to dig up information about Misti Ortiz. I found nothing, not even a Facebook page. The day dragged. Heat and few customers combined to sap any energy I might have saved from Jerome's coffee. I decided I needed a real break, and that could only mean spending time with my sister, Max, and keeping my promise to check out her band. That night I drove to the club where the Rakers were the house band.

The Boxcar Bimbo had an address on upper Larimer Street. Tourists bunched together in Larimer Square and LoDo, but they rarely ventured north of Twenty-First, a not yet developed area of warehouses, Mexican bus depots and other businesses that didn't fit the LoDo aesthetic. Homeless men and women congregated at the end of the block. Clubs like the Bimbo capitalized on the old Larimer Street skid row reputation and attracted customers who didn't care if the place was trendy, only if the music blasted away the daytime aches and pains.

The Bimbo stretched long and narrow. The squat building resembled a World War II bunker more than a boxcar. Nothing said bimbo until I got inside. The life-size inflatable doll with the perfectly formed oval mouth, Orphan Annie eyes, anatomical correctness and Betty Boop outfit greeted customers from the red leather seat of a chrome and black Harley. The plastic sex toy made me feel like I should avert my eyes out of respect for the lady's lost modesty.

An antique-looking mirror with a filigree frame extended behind the battered bar along one of the walls. Dolls of every size, color and condition hung from the ceiling, their ceramic, plastic and rag hands somehow fixed to the cracked tiles. A rotating light rapidly changed the color of the few tables and chairs scattered around the floor and the people sitting in them. An overflow crowd filled the club with noise and smells. A few years before, cigarette smoke would have clogged the air and my sinuses. The unrelenting noise agitated me.

I didn't see a face I recognized. The customers' youth struck me. I felt out of place and too old for my surroundings. I could deal with feeling out of place. I had trouble with the "too old" thing.

Max's band played in the club four nights a week, starting around ten. I hadn't heard the latest version of the Rakers, which she reminded me of at every chance. Max preferred to stay back stage when the Rakers entertained. She worked hard as the band's manager. On a gig she had to deal with numerous details and crises. Occasionally she joined them on stage with her tambourine or to wail a song whose lyrics I never understood. The last time she talked to me about the band, she said she was changing a few things I might like.

I managed to squeeze up to the bar and hollered an order for a Dos Equis. The bartender delivered quickly and I thought she said "three dollars," which I set on the inner lip of the bar. The hum of people surrounded me, choked off the air. The beer soothed my anxiety. I left the bar and walked to the far side of the club where the band set up. The musicians bounced around the stage while they checked their instruments—three guitars and a drum outfit.

A part of the crowd mingled in front of the stage. I moved in as close as I could. Maxine did not appear on the stage or in the background.

The lights dimmed. A spotlight focused on the band—four young men with beards, filthy jeans and not a hint of a smile. One guy's head was bald, another sported a spiky red hairdo, and the other two had greasy shoulder-length locks. Without any introduction or build up they began to play. Immediately the sound level shook the walls. My feet jumped from vibrations in the floor. The audience gyrated, shook and bumped in the tiny space that served as a dance floor.

I hated the song. Nothing but noise. I liked most music, even some country. But the Rakers hurt my ears. I stuck with the band, finished off my beer, then walked back to the bar. Glasses hanging from a wooden rack behind the bartender rattled and tinkled. I secured another beer and walked in the opposite direction from the stage.

"Hey, where you going?!" Max shouted her greeting, but I heard only some of her words. I'd walked right past her in my escape from the harsh decibels.

"I can't hear anything," I shouted back. "Where can we talk?" I pointed at my ear and shook my head.

"Come with me. Sometimes you act like a helpless child."

I followed her to a narrow staircase near the restroom doors. She wore flared jeans, a bright red silky blouse and enough jewelry to sink the Titanic. A butterfly tattoo adorned one shoulder. She climbed the rickety stairs to a level of the club that I hadn't noticed. The temperature increased but the noise dramatically decreased. Another crowd of people took up the second floor but they were quieter than the first-floor mob. Max found us a booth.

"You didn't like it, did you?"

"Just not my thing. That's all. You got a great crowd. Someone likes your band."

"We do okay. Steady dates in several venues. The boys are happy."

"I thought you were doing something different?"

"We are. But that's not for the public yet. You won't believe where we're going with our music."

"Tell me. I need to hear how someone is doing what they want and feeling good about it."

Before she answered, a woman tapped her on the shoulder. Max jumped up and hugged the stranger. Then they kissed with a show of affection that signaled Max had herself a new lover.

When they unlocked their lips, they continued to hold hands and sat down.

"This is my brother, Gus. I hoped you'd meet him tonight."

The woman stretched her hand to me and I shook it. About a dozen silver bracelets jangled on each wrist. Heavy eyebrows and bright teeth accented her dark skin.

"I'm Sandra, Sandy. You look a lot like Max."

"Thanks. That's a compliment."

"I meant it that way." She glanced at Max. "Your brother's cute."

"In a hoodlum, lowrider way," Max said.

"Hey," I said.

"Just kiddin'. You know I love you, bro. You're the best."

"Now you're making stuff up."

She smiled. "Seriously, Gus. You're family and you've always put the family first. You stood by me. That's big in my book."

I got a little choked up.

"I can't wait until you meet my brother," Sandy said.

"He here in Denver?" I asked.

"Afghanistan," Sandy said. "Nine more months. I haven't seen him for two years."

"To your brother," I said. We each drank from our beer. "You two been together for long?"

The question sounded rude but I didn't intend to be impolite. I needed a point of reference. Max's relationships tended to burst on the scene and then fade out. I wasn't one to talk, but lack of commitment plagued her like bad luck stuck to me.

"For a few weeks now," Sandy said.

"We met last year," Max said. "In Austin at South by Southwest. She checked out the Rakers because they were from Denver. I had to go all the way to Texas to meet someone from my own hometown."

Sandy reached over and kissed Max again. Another deep one that made me look away.

"Maybe I should give you two some privacy," I said.

They reluctantly let go of each other.

Red blotches of embarrassment or emotion or something crept up Max's cheeks and into her forehead. "Sorry, Gus," she said. "I know you don't like PDAs. You're such an old man sometimes."

They laughed and held hands again.

Max sounded cheerful, upbeat, like always. Corrine and I toted cynicism like sacks of potatoes. We were as close to clinical depression as we could get without requiring a prescription for Prozac. Max, on the other hand, represented the cheery side of the family. She was the only one on that side.

Max's good disposition did not come from a happy upbringing. Our father never accepted her coming out as a lesbian in high school. The final years of his life were hardest on her. He didn't disown her or anything dramatic like that. He simply never hugged her again. I doubt they said more than a dozen words to each other in the five years from her announcement to his death. I did what I could as her brother. I could never be her father.

I trusted her reliability and composure. I turned to her when I needed help but not another Corrine lecture.

I looked at Sandy. "You're a musician, too? Or . . ." I said.

"Sandy's my collaborator," Max said. "She's part of my new project. She's got a degree in music and can play at least three instruments, but she wants to produce. The band loves her and her ideas. I'm really excited, Gus."

"Great. That's all good. But, what is it? I haven't seen you this worked up since you won the four hundred meter dash at the district track meet."

"You tell him, Sandy."

Three more beers appeared from a mysterious hand that set the bottles on our table.

"We're sampling jazz. That's all. The guys are very talented. They can play almost anything. Steve's father's played in the Denver Brass Band for years. He grew up with that kind of music. Miguel started out with a mariachi group, if you can believe that. It's just incredible what Max has pulled together. Now they're adding jazz riffs and sentiments to the basic tonalities of the music they play, only, of course, in different time sequences."

Her words meant little to me.

"You're going to love it," Max said. "Very soon we'll have a CD ready for a demo. We just might end up with a recording."

"Are you talking about real jazz?" I said. "Coltrane, Parker, Armstrong?"

They nodded. "Absolutely," Sandy said. "Although not so much straight-ahead or be-bop. More fusion."

"*Bitches Brew*, Gus," Max said. "Can you believe that? My guys are working with Miles Davis' masterpiece."

"Whoa. How's that going? That's got to be complicated."

They nodded again. "Absolutely," Sandy said. "Complicated, intricate and difficult. But these guys can do it."

I listened to a few seconds of the music from downstairs. I shrugged. "It might fit in. I guess. You'll have to share it with me when you're ready."

Max grabbed my hand and squeezed it. "You know I will, Gus."

I drank more beer. Max and Sandy couldn't keep their hands off one another.

"Max tells me a friend of yours was killed?" Sandy said. "That must be terrible."

"Not a friend, but I knew him for years. Someone shot him."

"The cops have been questioning Gus," Max said.

"Really? They think you had something to do with the shooting?" Sandy said.

"They don't know where else to look, that's all. I saw the guy who got killed the day before he was shot. So, yeah, the cops talked with me. But, it's nothing."

"Who was he?" Sandy said.

"Arturo Baca. A real estate agent. He made a lot of money on North Side development."

"Artie Baca?" Sandy said. "You knew him? I heard on the news about them finding his body. Small world." She scratched at the label on her beer bottle.

"Why you say that?" I said.

"Oh, it's only . . . it's that . . . "

"What is it?" Max said. "Now you got me curious."

"No big deal. Artie Baca helped my mother sell her house when the old man died. We both wanted out of there as soon as possible.

Too many bad memories. He did it quick and Mom made some money."

"Recently?" I said.

"Yeah, about a year and a half ago. He would talk with Mom occasionally, after we moved. She thought he was a friend. I did too, until he hit on me. He quit calling when I told him I had no interest."

"Yeah, that's Artie," I said.

"Then, out of the blue, I saw him, not long ago, leaving this place. He was toasted. Could barely walk."

"Artie Baca was here?"

Sandy nodded. "Absolutely. Not his usual hangout, for sure. He wasn't alone. A girl partied with him. Too young for the bar, but no one hassled them. Pretty little thing. She helped him, held him up so he wouldn't fall over."

"You're right," I said. "It really is a small world."

"There was something funny about that whole scene."

"What do you mean?" Max said.

"I was outside, getting some air."

"Is that all?" Max said.

"Don't get weird on me. This was before you and I hooked up, but I wasn't doing anything except trying to breathe fresh air." She smiled at Max and Max returned the gesture.

"So, what happened?" I said. "The girl took Artie outside, and he was drunk. Then what?"

"She pushed him into a nice car in the lot. More like threw him. Then she climbed in the back seat."

"She didn't drive?" Max said.

"No, that's what I noticed. She got in the back, Baca in the front. This huge Mexican guy, wearing a cowboy hat, sat in the driver's seat. He started the car and they drove away. I guessed Baca had a chauffeur or a designated driver. It felt strange."

"That all that happened?" I said

"Only that I heard Baca say to the girl, before he passed out, that she should call a taxi. But why'd he say that if he had a driver?"

"As though he didn't know he had a driver."

"Exactly. Maybe he was a friend helping out, or the girl called him instead of a taxi. I guess there are explanations. I hadn't thought about any of that until I read about Baca's killing."

The downstairs crowd roared when the band lit into a club favorite. Somewhere in the din I heard bits and pieces of "Light My Fire."

"Come on, Sandy," Max said. "I should be downstairs with my boys. Let's dance. Gus?"

"Go ahead. I'm ready for another beer, then I'll take off. I'll call you, Max." She hugged me and kissed my cheek.

"Good night, Gus. So happy you made it tonight."

"It's been a pleasure, Gus," Sandy said. "I expect we'll be seeing more of each other."

They rushed downstairs. I sat at the booth for a few minutes before I left. Sandy's bumping into Artie and Misti was nothing more than a coincidence, but it got me to thinking again about them and the unknown driver.

"Too many unknowns," I said.

A kid with a Mohawk haircut grunted at me. "What'd you say?" I shook my head. "Nothing. Talking to myself."

I left the bar and drove to my back room. On the way I passed a group of men standing at a corner, setting up cardboard shelters and newspaper beds. I looked away but the scene caught in my throat.

At Sylvia's Superb Shoppe I made sure I had clean clothes for Artie's funeral.

9

The only suit I owned, a dark blue pin-striped job with out-of-date, too-wide lapels, felt warm and itchy. Many people at Artie's funeral didn't wear suits or sport coats, not even ties. I wasn't like that. I believed that death deserved respect and the best way I knew to give respect was to dress like the occasion mattered, which meant that I sat in a pew under too many layers of clothes.

Judging from the mourners in the old Catholic church, Artie circulated within a wide and varied circle. Many were friends like me—blasts from his past and misspent youth. We wore the funeral look, stressed and worried, that said, "How much time do I have left if Artie's gone already?" Several realtors, lawyers, bankers and developers represented the money crowd. These men and women dressed neat and professional, nothing out-of-date about their outfits, but stress and worry played on their faces, too. Deep down, under the uniforms and costumes, we all harbored the same fears.

After the services, Linda Cisneros Baca, the widow, kept her children close and accepted the condolences of the crowd outside the church. An older woman in a faded black dress huddled near Linda and the children—Artie's mother, I assumed.

Artie's body rested in the hearse and the procession to the cemetery waited for Linda, the children and the mother. When I had the chance I walked up to her and extended my hand.

"I'm very sorry, Linda. If there's anything . . ."

She pushed away my hand and gave me a quick hug.

"Gus Corral. Thank you for coming. It's been too long. You and Artie used to be such good friends."

"Yeah," I said. "There's never enough time for old friends, is there?" She nodded then moved on to the next person in line.

Linda appeared to be holding up well. In high heels and a simple black dress, she towered over many of the people who commiserated with her. A few strands of gray punctuated her dark auburn hair. Tiny wrinkles floated around her mouth. Blood-tinged eyes betrayed her calm exterior, but she radiated health and vigor. She kept her back straight. Her long neck stretched taut under her clenched jaw, and her legs looked sinewy and toned—a runner's legs.

Her daughter and son stood behind her. The boy seemed angry, the daughter cried quietly.

I started to say something to the older woman standing next to Linda. She cleared her throat and whispered, "Gracias." Her rheumy eyes didn't look at me. Occasional sobs escaped her throat. I walked on to my car.

I followed along in the funeral procession to the cemetery where the mother completely fell apart. In Spanish she let out her anger in loud curses and threats against God and whoever was responsible for her son's death. When the coffin was about to be lowered into the ground she screamed. Two men gently moved her away. Her sorrow filled the air and cascaded across the dark green lawn. Linda drew her children closer and waited with them until Artie's coffin disappeared. She led the son and daughter back to their car, her arms wrapped around their shoulders. The girl looked back at the burial site. Linda and the boy stared straight ahead.

The scene messed with my head. My throat tightened and a swirling uneasiness took root in my gut. I attributed the nausea to the general effect all funerals have on me, with the added touch of the connection to Artie.

It's not like I had any special reason to feel sorry about Artie. His surprise visit was the first time I'd seen him in years. The only motive he had for talking with me was to rope me into his plot to get rid of his blackmailer. Other than that, Artie Baca hadn't any use for me since we were arrested together, hundreds of summer nights ago.

But I couldn't ignore the hysterical mother and the grieving children and the essential waste of Artie's life.

I didn't spend much time at the grave. I said a fast prayer, maybe for Artie or maybe for me. Then I waited in my car. When other cars started up I drove to Artie's house, a nice place near Sloan's Lake about twenty minutes from the cemetery. Southwestern furniture, Indian pottery and bright wall colors complimented the Southwestern architecture. An amazing picture window took up most of the front wall of the house. The Baca family had a great view of the lake, picnickers and boaters. The lake reflected mountains, skyscrapers, trees and homes. I imagined that at night the scene impressed as well, especially with the city lights mirrored in the murky water of the lake.

I wandered through Artie's house and jealousy got the better of me. We were the same age, we had graduated from the same high school, neither one of us had gone to college. He lived in one of the nicest houses in a very nice neighborhood. I camped out, literally, in the back of a second-hand store. Men and women with money and influence appeared upset at his death and their grief looked genuine. I couldn't get a half-hearted "good morning" from my ex-wife. Artie enjoyed the good life with a beautiful wife and handsome kids and enough money to afford paintings or sculptures or jewelry from any Santa Fe gallery. I had no kids, I drove a used and noisy Subaru, and any extra cash I managed to hold onto at the end of the week went for a few beers at the Holiday or another dive just as bad.

Then I remembered that I was alive and able to check out Artie's house while lucky Artie relaxed in the warm earth, minus critical parts of his heart. I told myself again that I did feel bad about Artie. I turned off the envy.

I settled in on the back patio among a group of people who attended North High with Artie and me. I didn't recognize most of them but two were too familiar—running partners from the years when one of the most important decisions I made involved picking my friends.

"Yo, Gus, how the hell are you, old man?" Tony said, or Shoe, depending on the mood of the evening. Tony Vega managed to be something of a star on a basketball team that couldn't win more than two games a season.

"Shoe, good to see you."

We semi-hugged and patted one another on the back.

"Too bad it's under these circumstances, eh?" he said. "Real sorry about Artie. What a trip, eh?"

"You mean that he was murdered and the cops don't know shit about what happened?" Ice said. Every mob had an Ice back in the day. David Zamarippa, legendary music man—he could sing, play the guitar and dance like Michael Jackson when that meant something. I liked Ice, even though he was an Oakland Raiders fan—I never understood that—but he'd left town to find fame and money in the music business. I heard that he returned and now worked for the City and County of Denver, taking care of parks in the summer and driving a snow plow in winter, when he wasn't on furlough. The City struggled with a budget crisis and guys like Ice paid the price with fewer hours and thinner paychecks.

Ice and I followed through with the same hugging, back-patting ritual.

"The cops will nail someone for this," Shoe said. "Artie is, was, a player. Look at this house."

"Player is right," Ice said. "You know how he ended up with this? He played suckers in the housing racket. He had a perfect in with his real estate license. He arranged loans that people couldn't pay from lenders who didn't care as long as they made a quick buck. Then they foreclosed. That's what happened here. Artie had the inside track."

"He picked up the house for a song?" I said.

"Oh yeah," Ice said. "He did that kind of favor many times for his pals downtown. When the housing shit hit the fan, Artie was one of the guys who made money. Him and his friends."

"They can't let his murder go without an arrest," Shoe said. "Now if it was you, Ice or Gus there, well . . . "

"Or you, pal," added Ice. "Far as I heard, you ain't caca either."

"Whoa, man. I got it made, you ain't been told?"

"No, I ain't," Ice laughed. "How about you, Gus? How you been? We never see you anymore."

"I don't get out much. Can't afford it. In case you haven't noticed, the economy sucks."

They both nodded and their faces turned all serious for a sec.

"Somebody told me you work for Sylvia. How's that going?" Shoe asked me and he must have thought he was sly, but a smile crept into his words.

Tony dated Sylvia before she settled for me. I'd assumed he'd taken her out after our divorce, maybe before, for all I knew. He had to be wise to all the dope about Sylvia and me and our current arrangement. One thing I did know was that there was plenty I didn't know about Sylvia and the breakup of our marriage. Except that I screwed up.

"It's all good. Meaning I don't have to see Sylvia that much. I manage her shop, supervise sales, keep the books, handle the marketing, take on extra help when we need it. I keep busy, that's most important to me."

Shoe and Ice glanced at each other and it was obvious we all knew I was full of it. But these guys were my homies—they didn't say anything. They'd been through their own hard times, and one thing we didn't do was kick a brother when he was down, unless it involved a woman, of course. That goes without saying.

Shoe brought the conversation back to Artie. "What do you think happened? I mean, for Artie to get shot like that and then dumped like he was a sack of garbage? That's hard core. Someone really had it in for him."

"Artie was into funky stuff, so it don't surprise me," Ice said.

"Yeah, the guy jammed people," Shoe said. "I don't want to speak bad about the dead, so I won't. This isn't the time or place. I'll just say I'm not surprised either. You remember what Artie was like in school? Add a dozen years to that, a lot more money, and a lot more attitude, and you can see why someone might want to shoot him."

"I wanted to shoot him at North High," Ice said. He looked around in case someone else heard him.

"That's harsh," I said. We let it drop.

I explained how a pair of policemen visited me about Artie, and they didn't miss a beat.

"That's what cops do," Ice said.

"It's you, bud," Shoe said. "The notorious Gus Corral. Reason enough right there for the cops to stop by."

We asked about classmates. I mentioned that I had seen Isabel Scutti. They both shrugged. Isabel meant nothing to them.

Ice brought up the mess in Mexico City surrounding the theft of the holy shawl of the Virgin Mary. "Had to be an inside job," Ice declared. It was my turn to shrug.

"The animals are running the zoo," Shoe said. "But if this doesn't get the Mexicans to do something about the gangs, nothing will."

When Shoe predicted great things for the Rockies and Broncos and Nuggets, I knew it was time to leave. I said I had to bounce. They also decided to leave.

Shoe and Ice agreed to call me to set a time to hang out in lighter circumstances. Shoe really did want to speak ill of the dead and I figured it would take only a few beers to loosen his lips.

Just before we were about to part, I asked, "You guys ever hear of a shorty named Misti Ortiz?"

Ice shook his head and left.

Shoe thought for a few seconds.

"The name is familiar. There's a Mexican family with a daughter that goes by Misti. I use the term family loosely. Bad news. Mexican OGs—the dark side for sure. The daughter is too young for you, dude. Why you asking?"

"Nothing, really. Sylvia asked me about her." I didn't want to open up the can of blackmail worms to Shoe, especially at Artie's funeral. "She owes her some money, something like that, and now she can't find her."

"Syl owes Ortiz money, or the other way around?"

"Syl owes the money. For some stuff for the shop."

"Not good. You don't want to owe the Ortiz family any money. That can be unhealthy. But this must be somebody else. Like I said, the Misti Ortiz I heard about is young."

"Too young to sell second-hand clothes to Sylvia?"

"Well, no. But that's not something I think a teenager would do, especially one related to the Ortiz clan. They don't need to sell their clothes. They got other ways of making money."

"Yeah, I guess," I said.

We did an old-fashioned, regular handshake. Shoe left.

I looked over the crowd for Linda to say goodbye but I didn't see her. Many people had stopped by to honor Artie Baca and the house had taken on an awkward and out-of-place party atmosphere. Artie would have liked that, especially the fact that he had a good turnout.

I did see the mother, who sat in a recliner with a wet towel wrapped around her forehead. She mumbled to herself. I steeled myself and approached.

She whispered a jumbled prayer, in Spanish. When she opened her eyes I extended my hand. I wanted to make my exit quick and painless.

"Hijo!" she screamed.

I jumped backwards and tripped against a coffee table. I lost my footing on a throw rug that covered a portion of the waxed hardwood floor and fell flat on my back. The mother stood over me, crying and praying.

"Hijo!" she screamed again.

I held up my hands. "I'm not your son."

Linda appeared at her side. "Carlota, cálmate. That's not Arturo. He's gone. Calm down. Go to your room and rest. Take a nap."

Linda's son grabbed the old woman's hand. "Grandma, let's go. Come with me. It'll be all right."

The grandmother quieted. She hugged her grandson and let him lead her away.

I struggled to my feet, breathing again.

"I'm sorry, Gus. Carlota thinks she sees Artie everywhere. Any man the same age—any Mexican-looking man. She's having a hard time. Artie was her favorite."

"I never thought I'd be mistaken for Artie. Must be the haircut."

She didn't laugh, not even a smile.

"I'm the one who's sorry. I just wanted to pay my respects and say goodbye. I was leaving."

"Let me walk you to your car. We haven't had a chance to talk."

"Sure." I assumed she wanted to make amends for the mother's antics.

"We should talk, Gus. About Artie, of course. There are some things I want to ask you."

"Whatever I can do, Linda."

She grabbed my arm and we walked across her precisely xeriscaped yard: neat bushes, flowering cactus, clumps of grasses with hints of red and yellow, a path made of blue and charcoal concrete pavers that zigged and zagged around flowers, plants and insects. I liked that yard. In a way, it reminded me of my mother's garden and the hours I spent with her working the dirt, pulling weeds and moving the hose. Linda was nothing like my mother. Her pricey landscaping bore no resemblance to my mother's hard work, but I tricked myself and let the longing take over.

"I hadn't seen Artie for a while, you know." I decided to clear that up at the jump.

"That's what I thought. Then the police told me they found a check on Artie made out to you. That's one of my questions."

She dropped my arm and stopped in the middle of her front yard. Bees darted in and out of brilliant purple sage. A hummingbird flitted around a feeder.

"Why was Artie going to give you a thousand dollars, Gus?"

That damn check. Money I didn't want. Payment for a job I quit before I started. More trouble than it was worth. A thousand dollars of questions and suspicions from cops and a widow.

"Artie stopped by Sylvia's shop a few days before he, uh, he was . . ."

"He did? To see you?"

"Yeah. He wanted me to do some work for him. I said yes, but then later I changed my mind."

"He hired you? Doing what? Whatever it was, it couldn't have been any good. We both know he wasn't a boy scout. I hope he didn't drag you into one of his schemes. You changed your mind?"

"Yes. I decided I didn't like what he asked me to do. So I was going to tell him he should get someone else. But I never got the chance." Then I lied. "I didn't know he had already written a check for the job. Not until the cops told me."

She looked at me hard, doubting, not believing. Too many details didn't sit right. First Artie Baca hired Gus Corral—unlikely. Second, I had doubts about the deal after I had agreed to do it for a thousand dollars—even more unlikely. Third, she didn't know anything about the arrangement—did Artie let her in on all of his plans?

"What was it, Gus? What did Artie want with you?"

"Ah, Linda, I don't feel good about this. I don't want to cause any trouble. Artie's gone. Can't we just leave it there?"

A bee buzzed near my ear and I jerked away. Linda swayed backwards in reaction to my sudden move. I grabbed her and supported her until she found her balance. She wobbled, but under my touch her strength returned.

"Tell me, Gus. Don't I have a right to know? The police are looking at you. They think there might be a connection between that check and Artie's killing. I know that's crazy. I told them that. But they won't let it go. You may be in trouble. I can help, if you need it. I just want to know what Artie was up to. I'm his wife, you have to tell me."

Her voice had gradually reached a higher pitch. She bit her bottom lip and then chewed on the fingernail of her left little finger. Tears filled her eyes.

"All right, all right." I gave in. "But remember I had decided not to do the job. I couldn't go through with it."

She waited in the sun for my explanation. Then I lied again.

"Artie wanted me to spy on you. He wanted me to watch you for a few days, without you knowing. He wanted me to learn if you were having an affair. I guess he thought you were seeing someone else."

She puckered her lips then coughed into her fist. The cough turned into a snort, then a laugh. She laughed quietly, but she didn't say anything. She wouldn't stop laughing but the laughter was silent, kept within herself.

I left her like that. Then I heard a loud and harsh laugh coming from her. For the second time in a few days, a woman had laughed at me when I walked away.

10

I endured a sleepless night. I blamed my tossing and turning on the heat. That wasn't the reason but I grasped at anything other than the truth. I couldn't get the memory of Artie's funeral out of my head. The sorrowful images of his mother, his kids and his wife picked at me. The scents of dying flowers, dead insects and an old woman's shawl penetrated my dark room.

Around three in the morning, I recalled a small electric fan sitting on a shelf near the entrance. I hated to get out of bed because I could lose any chance of falling to sleep. The promise of air, however stale, circulating in the cramped back area nudged me. I wrenched myself from my cot and shuffled into the shop.

My face felt slick and warm and the skin around my nose and ears itched. Moonlight and streetlight shone through the front windows. I didn't flip on the lights.

I saw the fan at the same instant I heard the alley door creak open. I stooped down to the floor. A high-pitched whine filled my ears. Blood rushed from my heart to my brain. I had the sensation of seeing every used gadget, useless trinket and rusted memory in the shop, but I couldn't hear.

I strained for more sounds that would confirm what I thought happened—someone opened the back door of the store in the middle of the night, someone who did not knock or announce himself, someone who did not rush in after prying the door open.

I crawled to the entrance that separated the back room from the shop. The door remained open and I laid my face near the opening at floor level. I scanned as best I could. I saw my shoes near the legs of the cot and the trash can leaning next to the alley door. A slim ray of light cut across the floor.

The intruders' athletic shoes moved slowly from side to side. My eyes traveled up his dark pants and shirt. As best I could without moving my head, I tried to see his face. He moved about an inch to his left and hunched down. The light from the front and rear of the store framed him and I clearly saw his clenched jaws and a pencil-thin, neatly trimmed mustache. In his right hand he held a gun.

He shook his head, looked around the room once more and backed out through the doorway. The door closed. My hearing improved enough to hear footsteps along the back of the building. I ducked under my work table where I was out of the light but I could see through the front plate glass.

Several minutes passed before I saw him again. He walked to the front of the store, too casual. He brazenly stared into the picture window. He cupped his eyes and stayed like that for several minutes. Then he disappeared from view. I released my held breath and stood up. My back tensed from the awkward position I'd maintained under the table.

Headlights lit up the street and I fell to my knees. A car sped down the street.

I checked the back door for evidence of the intrusion but it looked the same—easy to jimmy open by anyone who understood the basics of cheap locks.

I shut it and locked it again. I moved a box of *Life* magazines against the door and felt relatively secure that the box would slow down the next intruder and give me a few seconds warning.

I crawled back on my cot. I had forgotten about the fan, my nightmares and Artie's funeral. I wouldn't sleep any better, but I knew that the guy wouldn't return, not that night anyway.

When the ringing phone woke me, I wasn't sure if I had dreamed about the mustachioed man with the gun, not until I saw the box of magazines propped against the door.

"Hello," I said, still not completely awake.

"Gus," Jerome said. "I have to talk to you. I found out a few things about the Ortiz girl. I'll be over in a half-hour. You gonna be there, at the shop?"

I hesitated. Jerome sounded too eager.

"Gus? Okay? We need to talk. Today."

"Why don't I come to your place? I could use a cup of coffee. I didn't sleep right."

"No, man. I can't talk here. I'll come to you, and I'll bring you some coffee. Laters."

He hung up.

The whine in my ears returned.

I paced around the shop for several minutes. I speculated on what Jerome wanted to tell me and whether he was somehow connected to my visitor from the night before. That was crazy. The intruder could have been anyone, a run-of-the-mill burglar, but my logic quickly crumbled into dust—the guy had been looking for me, he hadn't stolen anything from the shop when it looked like it was empty. He had to be tied in somehow with Artie.

I'd asked Jerome to get me information about the woman who tried to squeeze money out of Artie, a woman who could be a threat to me, although nothing I knew about her supported that guess except that she was part of a family of criminals. I easily jumped to conclusions about her.

Then my head went extreme with plots and subplots, all ending with Jerome having to shoot me because last night's hitter had missed his chance. Jerome would say he was sorry, say "nothing personal, bro, just business," right before he did me. I'd die with one word on my lips, "Why?" I would never know the answer.

I called Max.

"Geez, Gus," she said. "You never call except to wake me up. This better be good."

I didn't want to go into a long explanation with Max. She tended to minimize my anxieties when what I wanted was unquestioned support for my paranoia. For her own sake she should know as little as possible about my encounters with the recently deceased Artie Baca and the disappointed break-in artist.

"I have an appointment in a few minutes with Jerome, remember him?"

"Sure. I had breakfast at his place about a week ago. He asked about you."

Strange that Jerome hadn't mentioned seeing Max. Why not? I tripped out on that dead-end train of thought for a few seconds until Max snapped me back to our phone call.

"Gus? You still there?"

"Sorry. I thought someone was coming in the shop. I can't focus. I'm not sleeping all that great. Anyway, I'm meeting with Jerome. It shouldn't take long. Give me an hour. Say between eight-thirty and nine. I'll call you back then."

"What are you talking about?"

"Just go along, okay? This is important. If I don't call you back by nine, do me a big favor and call me? Okay? If you can't get me, come by the shop? Okay, Max?"

"What are you up to? You in trouble?"

"No, no. Don't worry. There's no trouble. I'm just being careful. Please, can you do this? Please?"

"Whatever, Gus," she said. "You're going to have to explain, in detail. I mean it."

"You're the best, Max. Love ya."

"Be careful."

I had a hard time waiting for Jerome. I couldn't sit still. I drank too much of my cheap instant coffee. I yawned over and over and had the jitters. I walked out of the shop several times, only to rush back inside in case he called the shop's number. No good rationale existed for me to doubt Jerome but that's where I was that day. Call me weak, crazy, whatever. By the time Jerome walked through the front door I felt wiped out and uptight. Nervous energy flowed through me like bad water.

He wore the same hat but a different version of the shirt he had on the last time I talked with him. He held two coffees in his hands. I had to hold the door open for him.

"Here's your cappuccino, bud."

I took the large Styrofoam cup with his logo—a cursive "Jerry's"—and set it on the table. He looked surprised.

"I thought you needed coffee?"

"Yeah, I did, but I drank almost a pot waiting for you. I'll drink yours later. Thanks."

He shrugged.

"What you got for me, Jerome? What can you tell me about Misti?"

I paced around my table and watched him. He took a long drink from his cup.

"You sure you want to keep on with this? I meant it when I said you should leave her alone. Misti Ortiz is nothing but trouble, Gus."

"Just give me a phone number or whatever the hell you dug up. I don't have all day." I was more abrupt than I intended but I couldn't control my mouth.

"Hey, man. Relax."

"Yeah, yeah. Sorry."

"Anyway. Her name is Marina María Ortiz but she goes by Misti. She's the sister of Lorenzo Ortiz. You ever hear of him?"

I'd read about him in a local weekly magazine but other than rumors about his gang connections, nothing from the article stayed with me. "Not much."

"Lorenzo's as much of a professional gangster as there is in Denver. He's involved in everything from drugs to gambling to you-name-it, including some very rough stuff, from what I've been told by guys who should know. He made his rep in Mexico, then migrated up north, where he got popped for drugs or guns, maybe both. He came out of prison five years ago tight with the Red Ones, los Rojos. A made man in that outfit. Now he's their number one guy in this region. His territory stretches from Albuquerque to the Nevada border up to Cheyenne and over to Kansas City, more or less. Denver's the center of his kingdom. It's a huge area for one guy to be the jefe."

Artie definitely screwed with the wrong girl.

"The Rojos are a unit of the Mexican gang run by Danny Ochoa out of Nogales. Small time, for now, but they're working on building up their empire here in the States."

He drank from his cup. I didn't like the way he looked at me. I noticed that his shirt had long-sleeves, and that didn't make sense. Not on another hot day. His pants pockets bulged with a cell phone, wallet and other lumps I couldn't make out. I remembered his ambition to make as much money as possible, never mind the risks.

"Lorenzo," he said, "who's also known as Carne, is a very important man. Anyone in his immediate family is also important. Meaning that his sister, Misti, is someone you don't mess with because that's the same as messing with Carne Ortiz."

"His nickname is meat?"

"Actually, it's Carnicero, the Butcher. The story is he gave it to himself in prison."

I liked the guy less and less.

"One other thing," Jerome said. "Misti Ortiz is only fifteen years old. I think that alone is enough to earn Artie a couple of bullets in vital organs. When I heard that, I lost whatever little bit of respect I had for the asshole."

I flashed on the video Artie had shown me. Only fifteen.

I mapped out a theory in my head about Artie that I thought I could pass on to Reese and Robbins. Artie got involved with the wrong woman, a habit he should have outgrown years before. Either Carne did not like the idea of Baca with his sister, or he didn't like the idea of Baca giving his sister a hard time about paying the blackmail. In any case, Artie paid the ultimate poon tax. It made sense to me. I had to find a way to sell it to the cops.

Jerome reached behind his back with his right hand. He struggled with something in his back pocket or the waistband of his pants. Without knowing I was going to do it, without any plan or idea what I would do next, I jumped him and knocked him down. I bent over him and slugged his nose. Blood immediately flowed.

"Motherfucker!" he shouted. He took a swing at me, but I dodged the blow. He tried to stop the blood from his nose.

"What the fuck? You're crazy. Look what you did to my shirt."

Blood splattered his shirt, pants and the floor. A few drops of blood stained his hat, which had managed to stay on his head.

"Stand up, slow." I grabbed a rusty golf club from a bag of old clubs that lay near the door. I dug out a handkerchief from my pocket and handed it to him. He balled it up and pressed it around his nostrils.

"Goddamn you. My nose could be broken. What's wrong? Why'd you jump me?"

"What you got in your back pocket? Turn around, yeah, turn around."

He turned and stopped. I didn't see anything that looked like a gun.

"What were you reaching for?"

"Jesus, that's why you hit me? It's a card with a phone number. You said you wanted to find out how to talk with Misti Ortiz. I was giving you the number, you son-of-a-bitch. You're going to pay for this, Gus. Count on it."

I took the card and saw the handwritten number.

"No way I let you get out of this without breaking an arm," he said.

"You got every right to be pissed, Jerome. Hurting me is not the answer. Heh-heh." I tried to sound low key, like I knew his threats were coming only from his immediate anger and that he couldn't possibly mean what he said. We had a history together that had to count for something.

The hardest thing I had to do in years turned out to be my apology to Jerome. I struggled with the words. I flinched whenever he moved. I went into too much detail about the break-in of the back room by the guy with the gun and how I thought the worst. I described my paranoia, my stress and my general fucked-up mood. I wasted my time. None of that mattered to Jerome. I reminded him of all we had been through. That only made the situation more tense.

"I'm a goof, Jerome. You know that. Whatever I need to do to make this up to you, I'll do it. I mean anything."

Jerome's nose finally stopped bleeding. I expected him to hit me the first chance he had but I put down the golf club. We stood a few feet from one another. There wasn't anything else I could say or do. I screwed up and Jerome had every right to pound my ass.

On cue, like the guardian angels they were, Max and Corrine walked in the shop. Max stopped with her mouth open. Corrine turned from Jerome to me and back to Jerome.

"Good God, Gus Corral," Corrine said. "What in the hell have you done now?"

//

That wasn't the first time my sisters saved me from a beating, or worse.

It helped that Jerome respected Corrine. I never doubted that Corrine's rep was solid all over the North Side, and Jerome was nothing if not North Side.

The best was that Jerome was sweet on Maxine. She let him down easy but one thing about Max, she knew how to get what she wanted. She had our parents wrapped around her little finger when we were kids, up until her coming out. Teachers loved her and let her get away with silliness that meant at least detention for the rest of us. She dropped onto the local music scene as the front person for the Rakers and quickly carved out a leadership role among edgy musicians, tough managers and flirtatious bar owners, even though her own talent was limited to banging a tambourine and occasionally singing for what passed as a slow song for the Rakers.

Max sized up the situation between Jerome and me and she did what she had to do for her older brother. First, to set the stage and butter up Jerome, she gave me holy grief for being an idiot, not holding back on any of the "how could you do this" or "what's wrong with you" or "you ought to be locked up." Then she tended to Jerome's bleeding nose, cleaned him up, offered him water and aspirin, all the while telling him the kinds of things that men like to hear from women who are taking care of them, things that their mothers told them when they were children, although they never would admit it. I wouldn't have been surprised to hear her sing, "sana, sana, colita de rana."

The scene made me nervous. She was my sis, the baby of the family who would forever be spoiled by her only brother. I had a hard time processing that she was her own person, and all that it meant. On that day, in an overheated second-hand shop with bloody rags piled in a corner, it meant easing the bruised ego and battered nose of a guy I knew as a hustler, petty criminal and con artist. A guy I punched only minutes before because I thought he was about to kill me.

I cleaned up the floor and Corrine helped, but the two of us stayed away from Jerome and Max. By the time Max finished, Jerome calmed down. He asked questions about my early morning visitor, Artie and Misti Ortiz, the whole mess. So that meant Corrine and Max heard everything. They had to ask their own questions. After about twenty minutes of trying to explain what had been going on, as truthfully as I could make it, I silently wished that Robbins and Reese would show up and arrest me. The third-degree from Jerome, Corrine and Max had to be worse than what the two cops could deal.

All three agreed that I should leave town for awhile. Lay low. Hide out. Go underground.

"That's easier said than done," I said. "It takes money to disappear, at least so that no one can pick up my trail without a lot of digging. Money? Ha. If I disappear, that makes me look even guiltier to the cops, when they should be watching Ortiz. I could go homeless, I guess, hang out at the shelter and food banks, but I don't think I can handle that. I'd rather face this guy and stop whatever this is." My hands gestured to include the entire North Side, the city, the world.

"And end up dead," Corrine said in her usual merry fashion. "You don't know when the creep will come back. He knows where you sleep, he probably knows all about you. Where you drink, who your friends are, even us." She indicated everyone in the shop. Max looked concerned.

"What I don't understand," Jerome said, "is what this guy wants. Yeah, he may want you dead, but why? You haven't crossed anybody, not lately anyway, and not enough to call in a trigger. So maybe he wasn't here to use his gun on you but he wanted to talk to you, threaten you, sure, or even take you to someone else. We don't know since you got out of bed at just the right minute, otherwise, we'd be having a different conversation." He sounded disappointed.

"I can't get over how you woke up just in time, Gus," Max said. "What if you had been sleeping when the guy broke in?"

"I didn't wake up just in time," I said. "I hadn't been sleeping. I moved out of the room at the right time, that's for sure. If I hadn't, then Jerome is right on. We would be having a very different conversation now—maybe I wouldn't even be here. Whatever was going to happen, I was awake when the guy chose to visit."

"Jerome's making sense," Corrine said. "What did that guy want? This has to have something to do with Artie Baca's killing. But you don't really know anything about that. You want to talk with Misti Ortiz to satisfy your curiosity, I guess, but is that enough for a man with a gun to show up in your room at three in the morning? No one but Jerome knew you were interested in Misti Ortiz."

"Except for the guys I had to talk with to get the number I gave Gus," Jerome said. "I had a hard time finding the info and somewhere along the line, someone easily could have leaked that I was nosing around about Misti Ortiz. Like I told this pendejo, this family and this woman are bad news all around. They don't like it when strangers start digging into their business."

"Ironic, no?" I used a word I thought Corrine would appreciate. "I wanted to talk with Misti Ortiz because I got a little shook up after I heard about Artie's shooting and the cops finding that check. I thought she might know something that could help me. My wanting to talk with Ortiz in my own defense caused the nighttime raid, precisely what I wanted to prevent."

Corrine shook her head. "You should have confronted the guy instead of ducking for cover."

Jerome smiled, Max winked. Ah, Corrine.

After Corrine and Max left, Jerome and I spent several uncomfortable minutes with each other. I apologized again but he cut me off. "Sorry" was not enough—he knew that, I knew that. I stood in front of him and waited with my hands at my sides, my eyes half-closed. He placed his hat on the table and bent down a bit, for leverage. When his fist hit my nose, my head spun around and I tumbled sideways. Instantly I felt the intense pain, a stinging, crunchy jolt that split my head and settled at the top of my skull. My eyes watered. Blood dripped from my nose. Not as much as had flowed from Jerome's nose, but enough to satisfy him.

I held my nose with a piece of towel from the sink in the back room. I bent over in pain. Jerome stood next to me for a minute.

"Damn, you Jerome," I said. "Damn me. Damn my nose. It hurts like hell."

"Welcome to the club. That's a start on payback, Gus."

"No, that's it. I paid what I owed you."

"Maybe. We'll see."

Another minute passed. I cursed again. He touched the bandage on his nose and grimaced.

"Come on, Gus," he said. "That's enough. You can quit with the play-acting. I got over it. You will, too."

"It hurts like hell."

"It's supposed to."

I opened my mouth but before any more swearing filled the air, I spit up blood. I coughed, then I choked up another cough that sounded like a laugh. I couldn't stop, and I laughed again. Jerome didn't laugh, but he eased up considerably. We both relaxed.

He sat on my red chair and talked about the phone number he had given me.

"It will connect you to someone who can put you in touch with Misti Ortiz. That's all I really know. I got it from a guy who works for Lorenzo Ortiz, and who I knew long before he hooked up with Lorenzo's outfit. I can't say more without putting that guy, and me, at risk. You call that number and play it by ear. Maybe you'll get to Miss Ortiz, more likely not. Either way, don't mention me, Gus. I repeat, these people don't fool around."

"Yeah, okay. Thanks, Jerome."

He picked up his hat, flicked his thumb at the spots of blood staining the crisp whiteness, sighed and said, "Laters, Gus. I've wasted enough time here." He walked out.

I didn't tell Jerome that I blamed him for my late night visitor. His old buddy, whoever that was in Ortiz's gang, must have talked about Jerome's interest in Misti, and that led to my visitor and our mutual bloodied noses. My nose throbbed and I had to keep dabbing at dripping blood. I quit feeling bad about hitting Jerome.

I pressed the numbers on my cell and waited. If my late night visitor was sent as a warning, I didn't get the message.

A man with an accent answered.

"Who is this?"

"I'm trying to get in touch with Misti Ortiz. I got this number from a friend who told me that this is the way to find her. Can you help me out?"

"Who are you, and what's your friend's name?"

"Look, I only want to speak with Misti Ortiz. Can you help me or not?"

He hung up.

I debated calling again but decided it would have been a waste of time. Jerome's information, and his bloody nose, had been for nothing.

I swallowed four aspirin and spent the rest of the morning staring at the street through the store's front windows. I waited for the man with the gun to show up again, or maybe a different hoodlum who would make sure I was at home before he barged in. I expected the two cops to stroll in again and pick up where they had left off. They were no-shows. When my stomach rumbled I remembered I hadn't eaten anything except coffee. I resigned myself to taking a walk to Chencha's.

My cell phone buzzed and vibrated. The readout said "unknown." I flipped open the phone and said hello.

"I understand you're looking for Misti Ortiz."

Not the same voice I had talked to earlier.

"Yeah, that's right. Can you help me?"

"This is Gus Corral, right?"

I almost dropped the phone. Hiding out suddenly sounded like a pretty good idea—Max and Corrine were right, again.

"That doesn't matter," I said, trying to sound in control. "I don't want any trouble. I just want to talk with Misti Ortiz about a friend. Maybe she can help me. I hope so, anyway."

There was a pause on the other end of the line. "You can't talk with Misti. You shouldn't have this number. I'll deal with that. But you can tell me whatever you want. I can answer all your questions."

"You sure? This is personal."

I heard a staccato, hiccup-sounding laugh. "I know all about Misti's personal bullshit, Gus. Don't you worry about that. You talk with me about anything relating to Misti."

"Not sure I can do that."

"Sure you can, Gus. Be surprised what you can do when you get incentive. But we can't do it on the phone. I don't like phones." Another pause. "I heard a little bit about you, güey. Need to put a face with a name, know what I mean? How about tonight, Gus? Come around to my club, about ten. Okay?"

"What club? Who do I ask for?"

That ugly laugh again. "The Midnite Oasis, where else? Tell the guy at the door that you're there to see Carne. Talk to the big guy with the bald head. He'll know what to do."

I heard a click and the phone call was over.

I called Corrine and told her what happened, that I was going to the club. She said some not very nice things about my brain power, but she resigned herself to my foolishness. Then I rang up Shoe and invited him to meet me at the Oasis around ten-thirty and to bring along Ice if he could find him. Shoe whooped and hollered, "Finally, a party!" Then he said how he hoped he could afford it.

I gave him a quick rundown about my late night visitor and my pedo with Jerome, which he took in stride by saying, "No shit? You know, I never liked that guy." I didn't say anything about my appointment with Lorenzo Ortiz. I should have felt guilty about not telling Shoe everything that was going on and for getting him into a potentially dicey situation, but, know what, I didn't. Not even a little quiver of concern for the guy who never let go of his crush on my ex-wife.

I snagged a carnitas burrito from the roach coach parked at the end of the block and chased it with two beers from my back-room cooler. The day sped by, faster than I wanted. I'm not sure what all I did except to get uptight again. I piddled around the store, walked around the block a few times, stared at sentences in a paperback. The digital clock flashed 9:15; darkness had fallen and I could no longer see the words on the page. I then chugged another beer and prepared for the biggest, glitziest and most expensive strip bar in town. I thought that if my meeting with Ortiz went the way I hoped it would, I would stay at the club with Shoe and Ice and spend some of my hard-earned and scarce money. If the meeting didn't go as planned, then Shoe and Ice could pick up the pieces, literally. A late night meeting with a guy whose nickname was the Butcher—what could go wrong?

A few years before, I was a regular at one of the strip dives just north of the county line. I gave that up, especially when money became a thing of the past. The club scene aged quickly and I found it less titillating each time I went back. I'd never ventured into the Midnight Oasis, but I'd heard about it. The best women, the best steaks, the best shows. Drinks pricier than the typical strip club mark-up. A twenty-five dollar admission and three drink minimum. Stories circulated about the back rooms, the VIP rooms, where anything and everything could happen, for a fee.

Lorenzo Ortiz had called it his club.

The Midnite Oasis throbbed like a neon bruise in the heart of LoDo, several blocks in lower downtown that served as Denver's boozing and partying Mecca for the suburban kids out for a thrill and the city kids looking to have fun at the expense of the suburban brats. That was my impression of LoDo. I didn't hang out there, even when I had enough income to splurge on drinking binges in sport bars and tiny dinners at trendy restaurants. But that was just me. The place attracted the Convention Center crowd as well as the tourists who stayed in the high-rise central hotels, which meant that the men in the audience, and a few women, had excess money to throw at near-naked, gyrating bodies while they drank expensive drinks.

I scrounged my back room for bills and coins, looked in my clothes drawers and under my cot, shook the Mickey Mouse and Donald Duck banks I had borrowed from Sylvia's inventory, and I came up with almost a hundred dollars. That wouldn't last long at the Midnite Oasis—enough for the required drinks and a few tips to the ladies, and then Shoe, Ice and yours truly would move on.

I locked up and exited through the back door. My car waited in the alley in the lone parking spot that came with the building. I dug out my keys and started to unlock the car. A pair of large hands clenched each of my elbows. I struggled to get loose but another hand covered my mouth. They doubled me over and I could not make any sound except a weak gasp for breath. They dragged me a few feet and then dumped me in the back seat of a car that smelled new. The leather seats were warm, almost hot to the touch.

Two brown bears sat at my sides. The rough-looking Mexicans dressed in dark shirts and black or tan cowboy hats. One of them said, "Be cool. Mr. Ortiz sent us to escort you to the meeting. Personal service, just for you."

I recognized the voice of the man who answered when I called the phone number Jerome gave me.

"I don't need the company. I got my own ride."

The car started and turned north when we came out of the alley. I thought I saw the cops' car, but it stayed parked on Thirty-Second. Reese and Robbins had not seen my sudden change of plans.

We drove away from downtown, further north. Street signs flashed by—Clay, Federal, Forty-Sixth, Fiftieth. I slumped into the seat and watched the night.

A few minutes into the ride, I said, "Lorenzo told me to meet him at the Midnite Oasis. You know the way? You lost?"

Again, silence.

"There are people expecting me at the Oasis. They'll know something's wrong if I don't show up."

The two guys squirmed in their seats. The one who had spoken before said, "You shouldn't have done that. Mr. Ortiz thought better about meeting at the Oasis. He can't be too careful, not with all his responsibilities. He's waiting for you at another place, quieter, less crowded." He stopped for a second, as though he was thinking over what he should say. "He might ask you to call your friends, so they don't worry, güey. Carne is like that, considerate."

The other guy in the back laughed so hard that he made the leather squeak. A black tattoo ringed his neck. It looked like a machete but I couldn't see for sure, and I didn't want to stare.

Several minutes passed. Total silence in the car. The men did not speak, no music played on the radio, and noise did not filter in from the outside. The smooth ride enhanced the quiet.

We turned into the parking lot of a Mexican restaurant near the Boulder turnpike in the city of Westminster. Casa de Mexico. I'd seen it many times but had never stopped—a large hacienda-looking building with a blue and orange tile roof, turquoise window frames, a red door, usually surrounded by pickups, sleek sedans and mini-vans.

The area where the restaurant was located contained brick ranch houses, strip mall businesses and schools with rolling lawns and asphalt playgrounds. A major highway ran next to sound-blocking fences that kept the houses semi-protected from the traffic. The streets extended from Denver and had the same names.

The driver took us to the back of the restaurant. He switched off the ignition and we sat in semi-darkness. No other cars were parked in the back and a six-foot fence blocked any view from the street. The restaurant gave off a glare of blue and yellow light that made the faces of the men who held me look like cartoon figures drawn in black and white.

I didn't see the man who had broken into the store. He wasn't one of the men in the back. When the driver turned around, I saw that he was clean-shaven with a light complexion, nothing like the guy who waved a gun at my empty cot.

A door opened and a band of light cut across me and my two guards. The men noticeably stiffened.

"Aquí viene," said the only man who had spoken to me. "Estén listos para algo con este tonto," he told his partners to get ready.

Lorenzo Ortiz climbed into the front. He turned around and looked at me. The meager light didn't reveal much but I could see that Ortiz had dark skin and a healthy head of hair. Hair cream reflected what light there was. His cologne filled the car with the scent of limes. His face had a definite resemblance to the photo of Misti Ortiz.

The three of us in the back crammed together. The other two were hefty guys with long legs and big feet and we couldn't move without banging into each other.

"I was looking forward to spending time at your club," I said. "This ain't quite the same."

"Yeah, maybe some other time," Ortiz said. "Right now, I need to know a few things. The sooner I know them, the earlier we call it a night. I'd rather be knockin' around with honeys than all these hairy men, entiendes?" His men laughed. "Who gave you the number you called today? What do you want with Misti?"

Lorenzo spoke quickly, slurring his words. He could have been high, or lazy. His thick accent made it all that more difficult for me to understand him, but I got the drift of what he said.

"Artie Baca gave me the number. When we talked about Misti. He said that was how he got hold of her when he wanted to . . . uh . . . visit. He thought I should have it, in case, he said. I never understood in case of what."

"Motherfucker," Lorenzo said.

He climbed halfway into the back and grabbed my left ear. He yanked me to him and slapped me, twice.

"You're lying, man. No way Baca had that number. Misti wouldn't give it to him. No way."

He acted as though he was going to hit me again. The men at my side grabbed my arms, doing their jobs, I guess. Lorenzo sat back in his leather bucket seat and the men released their grips.

"Yeah, you're lying, but that was good, what you said. Either you're smarter than everyone says, or someone is coaching you. It don't matter. Really. I'll find out who leaked that number. There's only a few who know it. It won't take long to connect the dots."

He turned around and faced the front of the car. "Now, what's this about Misti? What could you possibly want to speak to my dear sweet sister about? Mi querida hermanita. Little Angel I call her. She's just a kid, Gus. I could get the wrong idea, entiendes?"

I had to be careful how I worded what I needed to say. I didn't want to give Ortiz the wrong impression about me and my involvement with Artie, but I also didn't want to sound as though I knew too much.

"I wanted to make sure Misti understood that Artie and I didn't have any connection, and that I don't know why he came to me for help with the . . . uh . . . the payment. Truthfully, I was trying to protect my ass after I heard about Artie. That's all. I didn't want her or you to get the wrong idea, in case you decided you had to do something. . . ."

The man to my right snickered.

Lorenzo said, "You got a strange way of protecting your ass, amigo. Look around. You think I don't own your ass right now? You think you're walking away from this?"

"Yeah, I see what you mean. But, I don't know anything. I don't have any reason to care about Artie Baca or what happened to him. That's the truth."

Lorenzo still hadn't turned back to look at me.

"It's all good, eh, Gus? You're throwing around a lot of accusations, man. You mentioned a payment, like that should mean something to me. That what you're getting at? Do you think I deal in penny ante shit like blackmail?"

He paused and his men shifted in their seats, which I took to mean that they were readying themselves in case Lorenzo drew a gun and let me have it right then.

"But know what really bothers me, really burns me?" Now he turned. "It's like you're saying I can't take care of my sister. That if a pervert like Artie Baca was fooling around with my underage sister, you think I failed to do something about that? Are you trying to say

I can't protect my sister, my own flesh and blood? Are you saying I'm some kind of puto who can't handle his family business?"

"No, no. Nothing like that. I figure you do what you have to do. I'm only saying that you don't have any cause to worry about me. I don't know anything."

"Pobrecito Gus. For someone who don't know nothing, you go on and on. Bringing up blackmail, that was a mistake. Making it look like I'm into that, and maybe what happened to Baca? How does that sound to you, Gus? Like someone who doesn't know shit, or someone who knows just enough to be a pain in the ass?"

He said something in Spanish but I didn't hear him clearly. The door on the right side opened and Lorenzo's men dragged me out. They held me on the ground while Lorenzo stood over me.

"I'll do whatever I need to do for Misti," he said. "Don't worry about that, Gus. I think Baca knows that too." He walked away.

His men twisted duct tape around my mouth and I readied myself. Lorenzo stopped and hollered back at me. "Keep out of my business, Gus. Shut up about Baca. Stay away from my sister."

The beating started when his laughter bounced off the fence.

Lorenzo's men were quick but effective. If anyone from the restaurant heard or saw anything they kept it to themselves. I kicked the dirt and when my arms were loose, I tried to fight back, but my struggles were useless. I was semi-conscious when they finally dumped me in an alfalfa field along Lowell Boulevard, not too far from Regis University. One of them said he couldn't understand why Carne liked me. In other words, why was I still alive?

I tried to stand up and walk but that didn't turn out well. I threw up, teetered back and forth, and banged my knee on a rock, although another jolt to my body didn't mean anything. Nausea overcame me and I collapsed.

I slept in the field oblivious of the bugs and animals and anything else that sniffed me that night.

I didn't have nightmares about Carne and Artie and Jerome, didn't feel any pain, didn't cry in the dark. Not me.

12

When I finally woke up, dried blood covered my face, my ribs felt tender to the touch, and my shoulders burned like they were out of joint. I had a headache more intense than any hangover I ever suffered. But I felt good. In pain, yes, but good about everything else. Ortiz hadn't killed me. Big Fear Number One disappeared. Although he didn't come out and directly admit it, Ortiz made sure I and his crew knew that he could have killed Artie for messing around with his underage sister, so right there it all fell in place, like the puzzle pieces snapped together and a coherent, if messy, picture formed. My plan, such as it was, stood up to the first test.

I had a handle on the who and why, and that's all I really wanted. If Ortiz wasn't interested in eliminating me, then I could get back to my so-called normal life without waiting for more surprise visitors.

I sat cross-legged in the dirt. I soaked up the morning sun while I stared at the mountains off to the west. An early breeze cooled my dirty feverish skin. I thought that my gamble of talking with Ortiz had paid off even though his men had beaten me into a stupor and discarded me like a bag of trash along the highway. It was over, whatever it was. The second test of my plan required the cops. I could leave the loose ends to the police. I had to gamble that they were smart enough to pick up Ortiz's trail and follow through.

Morning traffic rushed over Lowell. The sun heated my back. Slivers of light bounced off windshields and street signs. My mind played tricks on me, the result of the aftershock from the previous night's activities, or hunger and thirst and a slight concussion.

Hazy blue mountains swayed in the early light, flat clouds raced across the sky faster than I had ever seen, and about ten yards from me a line of chattering quail moved as one through the knee-high grass and weeds. I hadn't ever felt like that before, but then I had never been threatened by a high-ranking gangster and treated to a coordinated attack by a trio of professional thugs, all in one night.

I couldn't reach a nagging itch in the center of my back and the more I tried to scratch, the more I grasped that at least one detail didn't quite add up. The man who broke into my room hadn't been part of the team that snatched me, then worked me over. But he must have been Ortiz's guy. I guessed he'd been sent to pick me up but had missed me. When I called Ortiz I walked into that talk all on my own. Ortiz must have punished his soldier for not doing his job. He could have sent the man to another city or state, banished for incompetence. The guy might have been permanently removed from the club by Ortiz. The nickname "Butcher" had to mean something.

Not my problem. I thought Ortiz would say something, but he had no reason to admit the break-in by one of his men.

I still had my wallet and some of the one hundred dollars. The change dropped from my pockets somewhere in the hectic night. Ortiz and his men had ignored my embarrassing life savings. I found my cell phone half-buried in the dirt. The battery indicator was low but I gave it a shot and called Corrine.

My sisters thought the worst when I didn't return to the shop that Saturday night and they couldn't find me Sunday morning. Corrine called several of her friends but no one had any ideas. They all backed off when she mentioned Lorenzo Ortiz.

"That guy is spooky," she said. "Men I've known for years, hard-asses and usually solid, clam up when I mention his name. Women I used to hang with didn't want to talk to me. This Ortiz has been building up quite a rep. News to me. No one wants to be involved with anything he touched. I really started to worry about you."

"Thanks," I said. "I was worried a little bit myself."

"I called Jerome and he gave me the same kind of push back. 'I warned Gus,' he said. Then he told me that you probably got what you deserved."

"That's cruel. But I can't blame him. He spoke the truth as he saw it."

When Corrine and Max accepted that there was nothing they could do about finding me, they quit calling people and turned to serious wine-drinking. They talked about their wrong-headed brother, our parents, Max's never-ending drama with her band and Corrine's failed romances. At two in the morning they crashed in the living room, Max on the couch and Corrine on her new carpet.

I recuperated by sleeping late for several days and eating too many blueberry and cream cheese empanadas from Panadería Santa Marta, the bakery next to Chencha's.

Sylvia came by the first afternoon and announced that she was leaving town on vacation so I didn't have to worry about the shop. "Take some time off," she said. "You need it."

She paid me in advance for two weeks and said I could open again when I felt better. I think she was worried about me and made up the vacation story as an excuse to help out. I could have asked, but I didn't want to open any doors that should stay closed for the good of both of us.

Max played nurse and tried to get me to a doctor, but without any insurance that was a trip I could not make. I didn't need any more bills, especially bills because of a beating. What could an Urgent Care clinic do for me that I hadn't already done for myself? Nothing felt broken and my bruises and swelling gradually retreated. Jerome's punch followed by the multiple punches from Ortiz's three stooges had been too much for the membranes and blood vessels of my nose and it periodically leaked blood for several minutes. That stopped eventually. Nothing I hadn't dealt with before.

On the third morning of my forced down time, I climbed the stairs to the upper level of the store, telling myself that I should finally get the floor fans. For years Sylvia had crammed her overstock into the single large room that made up the second floor.

That place gave me the creeps. Dust-covered boxes and large cobwebs filled the corners. Strange-looking gadgets that had no obvious purpose bumped up against one-armed and legless mannequins. Moth-eaten clothes hung on rickety coat racks. The lighting was bad and no way would I go up there at night. However, several streaked windows let in the sun without any problem, which meant that in the summer the place became unbearably hot.

The second story's balcony was its saving grace and the real reason for me to be up there. The wrought iron enclosure looked solid and an awning provided welcome shade. I found the fans and set them up in the store. I returned to the balcony and arranged a chair and a crate that I used as a table. I carried out a mug of instant coffee, the newspaper, my CD player and a couple of the Gold Medal paperbacks. I put on my shades. Gus Corral–on vacation.

I relaxed in the hot air and let my mind drift with the breeze. I tabulated my aches, bruises, where I hurt the most. I picked at the bandage that held my nose in place. I gave up on the coffee. I missed Jerome's cappuccino.

I'd always thought that I grew up and lived in the North Side. Nobody called it that anymore. I had become a resident of trendy Highlands, but that wasn't enough. My balcony perched in Lower Highlands, or LoHi, as the hipsters labeled the several blocks that more or less stretched from I-25 to Federal, bordered by Speer and Thirty-Eighth Avenue. Those of us who were natives to the area couldn't play that tune. We never used the name LoHi, a rip-off of the LoDo tag with the hope that the flash and cash of LoDo would somehow work its way up to LoHi.

Several new condos, already leased or under construction, obstructed the view from my perch. High density boxes were a booming business in Highlands—recession or not. My neighborhood had become fashionable and more expensive, with more traffic, more rude behavior and higher property taxes, according to Corrine.

Long-time landlords with run-down house rentals or duplexes could not resist selling to developers who, as soon as they had their names on the deeds, tore down the single or two-family homes to quickly replace them with multi-resident high rises that clogged the air, cleared out trees and animals, and blocked the view of the mountains. Newcomers without any long-term commitment to the area moved in, and the old neighborhood changed, big time.

When Corrine and I talked about the changes, I told her I had nothing against making a buck, even if I never learned how myself.

"I don't like what's happening to the North Side," she said, "and I'll tell that to anyone who'll listen. You can't make up your mind. You bitch about it, but you go along with it, too. What is it with you, Gus?"

"As long as no one I care about is hurt, then it ain't my business."

"So typical."

"Give me a break. The North Side is my home. For some reason, nothing I can pin directly, I do feel cheated, tricked, taken advantage of. I could have something to say about what happens around here, don't you think?"

"Not if you don't get involved. That's one of your problems. You care only up to the point that it means you have to act, or need to take time to do something about the situation."

I quit the conversation to avoid another lecture.

Artie Baca had been heavily involved in the transformation. He did well with the changes and, if I resented it, I had to admit some of that came from my envy of what he'd done with his life.

I shook myself out of my daydreaming and quit mulling over the changing scene. I quickly scanned the newspaper until I found two stories that caught my attention. The first made me realize that even if I tried, I couldn't escape the neighborhood makeover.

The article announced an open house and reception later that evening at one of the more expensive condo complexes, Quixote Plaza, only two blocks from where I sat. I could see its ugly façade and boxy architecture above the trees that cooled the sidewalks. According to the article, the development had been one of the late Arturo Baca's pet projects. The paper quoted Ralph Twittle, realtor, who first said that "Arturo Baca would have been proud of Quixote

Plaza. It's quite a dramatic change for this area." Then he admitted that "Highlands has reached a critical mass. It's gentrifying and gentrifying quickly."

His honesty sounded refreshing, although it made me queasy. I'd never be able to buy a place in my own turf. I thought about the older residents, the grandparents struggling to keep some trace of what their lives used to be but who now must feel like strangers in their own back yards. Or the families who couldn't keep up with taxes, increased mortgage rates, higher prices at the grocery stores, the generally higher cost of living that the gentry always brought with them. Those were consequences that I could blame Artie for and that I should have talked to him about that day when he stopped by the shop. As usual, I had kept my grumblings to myself.

The second newspaper story was darker and more intense, and it consisted of two parts.

First, a sidebar piece about the raging drug wars in Mexico that had claimed forty thousand lives, more than three thousand on the border alone, with some history and background of various criminals and their gangs. A highlighted box contained an ego-boosting gangster top ten list: the Zetas, Chapos, the Cartel, Los Rojos and others; Daniel Ochoa, Trinidad Morales and so on—a mug book of murderers, torturers, smugglers and thieves. The article did not mention Lorenzo Ortiz, but it noted that the gangs had begun to cultivate branches in several North American cities, including Denver.

The main part of the story had captured the world's attention for almost a week—the raid on the Basilica of Our Lady of Guadalupe in Mexico City and the theft of the most revered religious symbol in Mexico, maybe the entire Catholic Latino world. A ruthless group of gunmen killed ten people and wounded dozens during the attack—tourists, priests, nuns, food vendors— then seized the ragged cloak that framed the famous image of the dark-skinned, indigenous Virgin Mary, created by the Mother of God as a gift to the New World's converts back in 1531.

"They've gone too far now," I said out loud.

The shock and anger spread around the world. Thousands, maybe millions, of people reciting the rosary gathered each day at the basilica, in front of St. Peter's in Rome, and at hundreds of other churches on every continent. World leaders united to offer help. Every important official of every organized religion publicly prayed for the tilma and the victims of the raid. The pope issued special pleas and held continuous masses for the safe return of the holy blanket. Newscasters repeated rumors on television programs that the Catholic Church was willing to pay the ransom. But so far the thieves had not responded. The Mexican president vowed a relentless hunt for the stolen holy treasure and a crackdown on gangsters in general. He dedicated the remainder of his term to the "cleansing of Mexico and the extermination of the criminal elements that threaten the stability, the very existence of the Mexican nation." President Obama promised money, guns, FBI agents and heightened border security if the Mexican government requested assistance for tracking down the Rojos.

The raid on the basilica and the theft of Juan Diego's tattered wrap proved too extreme for some of the hardened smugglers and killers who had maimed, tortured, kidnapped and raped in their quest for the billions of dollars that could be made as narcotraficantes. Several Mexican gang leaders issued their own statements of condemnation against the Rojos.

I grinned at that bizarre mockery of common sense. El Cartel's chief, Trinidad Morales, in an on-air telephone call to a popular Mexican television talk show host, vowed to track down the Rojos, save the tilma and return it to the Church. I immediately thought the worst. The story confirmed my hunch. Unknown individuals had dumped Morales' body, minus hands, feet and tongue, on the steps of the Nogales police station. The detailed and massive tattoo of Our Lady of Guadalupe that covered his back, inked into his skin years before, appeared intact, untouched by his killers.

The theft, subsequent ransom demand and the execution of Morales were brutal and clumsy, and several government officials expressed amazement that the gang had orchestrated such a "daring, ruthless and suicidal attack."

I forced myself away from the blood and gore of the Mexican gangs and what appeared to be their all-out assault on civilization. It sounded surreal, fantastic.

I called Jerome. He didn't want to talk at first.

"I'm trying to run a business," he said. "No time for shooting the breeze."

"Take a break. You been at it since early this morning, right?"

"Maybe. So what do you want?"

"I saw the article in the paper about the robbery of Juan Diego's poncho."

"Forget the newspaper. Check it out on the Internet. Photos, videos, interviews with people who were at the basilica when it all went down. It's big news around the world. The heist turned into a bloody mess."

"Not planned very well, was it?"

"Well enough. They got away with the tilma, didn't they? It was a rough play, nothing smooth in the execution, but these gangs aren't known for their finesse. They shoot the place up, almost destroy what they are trying to steal, lose men in the getaway, and leave too many dead and wounded. Not smooth at all."

"Those people are crazy."

"Those people are your people, in case you forgot. Mexicans, dude. Killing each other by the thousands because North Americans need their daily fix and they're willing to pay exorbitant money for it."

"Mexicans, yeah, but not like any Mexican around here that I know. To rip off the Church goes way over the line."

"You don't know your history, Gus. How many thousands were killed in the Mexican Revolution? They even had a war against the Church. Lined up priests against the wall and shot them. That went on for decades, and who else did they kill back then? Pancho Villa, Emiliano Zapata, Madero. Those guys were heroes, legends. For some, they were as holy as the painted image of Mary on the peon's blanket. The killers, the killing machine, respected no one back then and nothing's changed today. One more chapter in Mexican history. Mexico's always been a blood-thirsty country. From the sacrifices on the pyramid altars to the serial killing of women along the border."

"At least Villa and Zapata died for a cause. What's the cause now? Where are the heroes today?"

Jerome laughed. "Some of these guys are looked on like heroes. There's songs about them, like the one about the poor kid from the slum who runs drugs across the border and gets rich by standing up to the man."

"Narcocorridos. Corrine plays them sometimes, when she feels more Mexican than usual."

"Songs about gunfights with the federales, or double-crosses, revenge ambushes."

"Wild West bullshit."

"It doesn't get any wilder than ripping off a religious symbol at least as powerful and respected as Christ himself."

"These guys try to come off as revolutionary outlaws," I said, "but you can't compare them to men like Villa and Zapata."

"The cause is what it's always been—money and power. The tilma got snatched because someone realized a lot of bucks could be made by stealing it. End of story. I gotta go." He clicked off.

I brushed away empanada crumbs that floated to the street. Below, four large noisy crows pranced on the curb. They strutted and screeched and argued over the remains of a squirrel that had been too slow for traffic. The scavengers pecked and backed off, pecked and backed off. Finally, the noisiest stretched his wings and raised his head skyward. He cawed loud and long and then flew off, a piece of squirrel meat hanging from his beak. The other three looked around for their foraging partner, and then they too deserted the picked-over carcass.

I was about to leave the balcony and call Shoe—I hadn't talked to him since we'd arranged to meet at the strip club—when a car parked on the street under my balcony. Detectives Reese and Robbins exited the car and banged on the shop's door. They looked in the windows, knocked some more, walked up and down the sidewalk. They never glanced upward. Reese tugged a card out of his jacket pocket and stuck it in the frame of the door. They returned to their car and drove off. I waited five minutes. Then I made my way through the hot and dingy second floor, down the dark stairs and into my room. From there I walked into the shop, opened the front door and retrieved Reese's card.

He had written a note on the back of the card. *Call me before it's too late. I can help you. Baca's not worth it.*

Reese could have meant anything. He was playing me, acting as though he had it all figured out. I doubted that he did.

It seemed simple. Follow up on the connection between Artie and Misti, which in turn should lead to Lorenzo Ortiz. If they were watching me they had to know about Lorenzo.

I could have called Reese and told him about Ortiz's admission that he had "taken care of family business." That would have been my death sentence. Lorenzo would need only two minutes to realize where Reese and Robbins got their information. I was the obvious source, now that I had revealed myself to Lorenzo. I had to walk a tightrope and keep out of it, but not let Reese and Robbins wander too far from the Ortiz family. The cops had to stumble around and harass me until they finally saw the light and targeted Lorenzo. They had to look like they did it all by themselves.

13

I called Shoe, who agreed to meet at the Quixote Plaza open house after six.

"I have a hundred questions," he said. "What happened? I've heard so many stories I don't know what to believe, and they're all crazy."

"I'll give you all the dope later. Bring Ice along, okay?"

I didn't call Reese. I figured he and Robbins had to be watching me and would show themselves when they needed to. Until then, I would go on with life acting as though I wasn't the center of curiosity for two cops who had zeroed in on me, even though it seemed clear all they had to do was squeeze Lorenzo Ortiz and they would have their case.

"They're the detectives," I said to myself.

I wasted the rest of the day—mainly by walking around the changing neighborhood. The evolution of the North Side was almost complete. Like the realtor in the paper said, we were at a critical mass. How could we fit in any more people? The work of all the Artie Bacas of Denver had paid off. For them. Some of us were left feeling like we'd been hit by one of those tornadoes that every once in a while threatened Denver.

The walk did wonders for my attitude. I still liked where I lived, changes and all. I saw people I'd known all my life, friendly, good people. I said hello to men working on cars, some bent over the engine, others flat on their backs on the pavement underneath their rides. Old women waved at me and smiled. They remembered my mother and father and believed because I came from a good family I must be a good man. I recognized elaborate gardens and barking pets, cedar fences that needed staining, cracked drive-ways—signs that some things always would stay the same.

I cleaned up the best I could in my makeshift shower, put on a blue shirt that Sylvia would approve of, and made my way over to Quixote Plaza a little before seven.

Several cars slowly circled the block. All the street parking was taken, the building lot did not have an empty space. About a dozen people loitered outside the fancy entrance to the housing complex. Inside, thirty-year old techies jostled even younger lawyers. Retired doctors gabbed with restaurant owners. A yoga teacher hung on every word from the district's city council person. The partiers stood elbow-to-elbow, butt-to-butt. I entered another world, far removed from my walk around the neighborhood, sucked in like a goldfish dumped in the toilet. Loud music bounced around the walls and ceiling. I couldn't tell what song was playing or even what kind of music blasted my eardrums. The heavy air moved around me. The AC hummed at max, and people shouted to be heard by the person next to them.

The housing market in Highlands stoked talk about an economic upturn. The average price for a home in the neighborhood rose in the past few years during the same time that housing in the rest of the city tanked. Everyone said it was a miracle and from the looks on the faces of the excited crowd in Quixote Plaza, the miracle couldn't have come at a better time.

The party spilled out from the first floor party room, adjacent to a covered swimming pool and a metal sculpture that, according to the silver plaque attached to its base, represented old man Quixote riding a horse. It looked more like aluminum springs and copper gears welded into a blue-green blob of no talent.

I grabbed a paper cup of red wine and strolled through the crowd. I saw what I expected—chrome and tinted glass and dark woods and potted plants and woodcut prints of the crazy Don and his sidekick, Sancho Panza, charging at windmills.

The potential customers looked like what I expected, too. I might have appeared a little out of my element but I did my best to blend in. That got easier when I saw Shoe and Ice huddled in a corner, clutching cups of wine in all four hands.

"Man, what are we doing here?" Shoe said.

"Free booze." I held up my paper cup to emphasize the point.

"Tastes like Kool-Aid," Ice said. Then he chugged what he had in one of his cups, which he promptly threw into a planter that held a fern-looking bush.

"Let's blow this," Shoe said. "We got better things to do. I want the DL about what happened the other night. Way it was told to me, you got your ass beat bad. You look like it, for sure."

Ice nodded in agreement. "Yeah, let's go. These things make me nervous."

"All right. I thought this would be interesting. Let me finish my drink and we'll hit it."

A tall woman in a red summer dress floated by and for a second I didn't believe she was Linda Baca. She circled the room next to an equally tall man wearing a white sport coat, turquoise pants and a pale yellow polo shirt. They stopped and talked with the realtor, Twittle—I recognized him from his picture in the paper. The three hugged, smiled, laughed. Old friends.

I finished my wine.

"So, we leaving or what?" Shoe said.

"In a few minutes. I want to check something."

"What could you want to check out here?" Ice said. "This ain't for us, bro." Ice had no patience.

"You see Linda Baca?"

Shoe and Ice looked where I pointed.

"Jeez—Artie's not even cold in the ground yet," Shoe said.

"She didn't waste any time, did she?" Ice said.

"That guy with Linda. You know him?"

Shoe and Ice looked at where I indicated with my empty paper cup. They shook their heads.

"Why you interested?" Ice said. "He a friend of yours?"

"In a way." I looked hard at Linda's escort, to make sure. He saw me staring at him. I thought he nodded at me.

"What do you mean, in a way? What way?" Shoe sounded irritated. He never could handle wine.

"He's the asshole who visited me the other night. The prick who busted into Sylvia's shop."

"You sure?" Shoe asked without taking his eyes off the man in the white sport coat.

"Oh, yeah. I'm sure. I think I'll ask Mrs. Baca what the hell is going on."

Shoe and Ice grabbed me before I could take a step.

"Easy, Gus," Shoe whispered in my ear although no one could have overheard us with all the noise in the room. "If he was looking for you, he might be the one who shot Artie. Linda Baca's all over him. What's up with that?"

"He never saw me. Far as he knows, I don't have a clue that he was in my place. Let's see how they act when I stick my face in theirs. This could be good. Come on."

They followed a few steps behind. Linda and her man saw me coming. Once I was about a dozen feet from them, the guy made like he was leaving. I ran up and grabbed him by the arm.

"Hey, what . . . ?" he said.

Linda shoved my hand away from her friend. "What do you want, Gus? What are you doing?"

"I think you owe me an explanation."

"If this is about the other day," she said, "I'm sorry I was so rude."

The sweat rose through my skin. My throat tightened. My plan to play it slow and force Linda and her mystery man to take the first step in a little cat-and-mouse dance didn't last long.

He squeezed closer to me and stared in my face. A few lines of gray streaked his hair but his mustache shined pure black. "I don't know who you are but I sure don't like your manners. Answer Linda's question, what do you want?"

Shoe and Ice maneuvered behind the guy. When he realized he was surrounded, he flinched. He stepped back a few paces.

"Why don't you explain what you were doing in my place at three in the morning? You or Linda want to get into that?"

Linda stood outside the small circle created by Shoe, Ice and me.

The stranger in the colorful clothes lost the color in his face. He looked over at Linda. She smiled, weakly. A worry line creased her forehead. We waited for a long few seconds. He said, "Screw you," and tried to rush past us. Shoe grabbed him and pushed him back toward me. They bumped into others in the crowd, prompting a few curses and return shoves. A ripple of tension shuddered through the crowd. Leave it to the locals to cause trouble.

Linda's friend stood a few inches taller than me and my pals. When he took off his coat and handed it to Linda, we saw his pumped-up biceps and chiseled chest stretching his yellow shirt. The noise in the room faded away. The crowd gathered around us. Before we understood it completely, we were outnumbered and lost our command of the situation.

A pair of security guards hustled toward us.

Linda stepped between us and waved away the guards. They ignored her and kept coming.

"Not sure what this is about," she said, "but if you want to talk about something, you know how to reach me."

"Oh yeah. I want to talk. With you and . . . "

"Right, you haven't met Artie's business partner, Raymond Olivas. He's an old friend."

The guards separated Shoe, Ice and me from the others. The guard who looked to be in charge said, "You need to leave. The party's over for you." He turned to Linda. "You okay, Mrs. Baca? These guys giving you trouble?"

"No," she said. "It's nothing. No one has to leave. Right, Gus?"

I tried to match her poise. "Yeah, no problem. Actually, we're leaving anyway."

Olivas offered his hand. I was surprised but I shook it.

"No problem," Olivas said. His hand clenched mine and squeezed for a few seconds too long. When I let my fingers go limp he released his grip.

The crowd melted away. The five of us stood awkwardly in the middle of the room under the watchful eyes of the guards. Shoe,

Ice and I walked toward the door. Linda and Olivas kept smiling, nodding their heads. They huddled together and whispered in each other's ears.

"We should've jacked him up," Ice said. "He violated your space. You can't let him get away with that."

The two guards followed us.

"Easy, Ice," I said. "We're about to get thrown out by security, and who's going to believe that Olivas broke into Sylvia's shop? We walk now, and I try to put this together. Maybe I'll give Detective Reese a call."

I started through the wide glass doors when I saw Lorenzo Ortiz and two of his henchmen walking up the steps. I let them pass. Ortiz watched me through eyes reduced to slits as though the light from the party was too bright. His men waited for a signal about what they should do. He raised two fingers in a V—the old peace sign—and motioned for his men to keep moving. The older guard high-fived Lorenzo and shrunk against the wall to give him and his crew plenty of room. Twittle rushed over to shake his hand. Linda and Olivas waited for their introduction. Everyone smiled.

"I need a drink," I said.

14

I found that drink and several of its pals. Shoe and Ice tagged along on my one-track slide into inebriation. They managed to keep up with me for most of the night. Denver has some sleazy bars if you know where to look, and we looked hard.

The booze and earlier drama from the Don Quixote fiasco had me wired, not to mention the overall stress since Artie visited me. Shoe and Ice heard about my troubles with Lorenzo Ortiz, the police and how Artie Baca infected my life with his peculiar brand of poison. I held back before I spoke about my adventure in the expensive ride with the new-car smell. No way for me to tell that story and not look bad. They weren't satisfied and got most of it out of me. Liquor loosened my tongue and I couldn't shut up. Shoe and Ice hung on every detail of how I ended up in a restaurant parking lot rather than the strip club. I said too much but they weren't likely to remember the finer points of my tirades.

When I finished, they bought me a shot and toasted my survival.

"Lorenzo more or less admitted that he took care of Artie," Shoe said.

"He didn't admit nothing. Ortiz was only protecting his rep with his men," Ice said. "He never clearly said it, did he? If he did the job on Artie, why not take care of Gus, too? Gus is going around making accusations. Foolish, but that's Gus. You'd think the Butcher would want to shut him up. You're lucky you got nothing more than a beating."

"I don't feel lucky."

Shoe had a different take. "Ortiz doesn't need to whack Gus," he said. "Gus doesn't really know anything. He explained he was only covering his butt to make sure there was no misunderstanding about his role with Artie. Right, Gus?"

I nodded.

"Our friend here needed to clarify that thousand-dollar check," Shoe said. "Now that's been done, and Ortiz moves on to bigger fish. He accepted Gus' excuse, and he gave Gus a direct and painful warning. That should be enough."

Ice didn't buy it.

"I ain't no Sherlock," he said. "But if the City and County of Denver paid me to look into shootings and other crimes of violence, I sure would spend a lot of time with Artie's old lady. Open and shut. What's the names of those two dicks that questioned you? We ought to call them. Better yet, Crime Stoppers. Get the reward."

We lifted our beers to that idea.

"It's too obvious for the cops," Ice said. "They'll never figure it out. Without someone confessing they don't know how to solve a crime. I'm just sayin'."

"I don't think she did it," I said. "With the way divorce goes these days, she had no reason to shoot her way out of her marriage. A lawyer's all she needed, not a gun."

"You're assuming Artie got killed over money," Ice said. "You know about crimes of passion? Say he pissed her off real bad, for whatever reason. Odds are another woman's in the picture. Or she's tired of taking his crap and putting up with his knocking her around. You know how he was. We're talking about Artie Baca, remember? She lost it and capped him before she knew what she was doing. I can see her pumping bullets into Artie for all the years she didn't fight back. Then, her boyfriend helped her cover it up."

"Hate to admit it," Shoe said. "That makes sense."

"Could be," I said. "But I still like Lorenzo Ortiz. More in his character and line of work."

We were in a place called the Silver Key, another new club on Thirty-Eighth that hadn't settled if it wanted to carry on business as a yuppie sports bar or a neighborhood joint. After the tour of dives we had been on for most of the night, the Silver Key seemed almost upscale. We couldn't handle it—too much alcohol accumulation by the time we walked into the place—and not only were we loud and obnoxious, we didn't know anyone. A couple rounds of microbrews and shots and we must have tipped the balance in favor of the yuppies.

Shoe looked like he could still captain a full-court press.

"How you stay in shape?" I asked. "Playing ball?"

"Not so much. I run every day, through the streets, usually between Lowell and Tejon. No gym for me, except maybe in winter. Love it."

"That's good," Ice said. "Keep moving. Stay healthy."

"You ever see Linda Baca on your runs?" I said. "She's into physical exercise."

"She looks like she could handle herself," Shoe said. "There's always runners on the streets. If she was one, I didn't notice. I tend to zone out when I run."

"That'd be trippy, if you and Linda ran together," Ice said.

"No way could that ever happen," Shoe said. "Different crowd. Let's get another round."

Drinking with my old friends triggered the usual nostalgia and regrets. Classic reasons to drink in the first place. Ice and Shoe had been part of my life since the time I started to keep memories. Each one brought something different to the table.

During various times of the night I recalled that Shoe carried a torch for Sylvia, but in my more lucid moments I understood how it didn't matter. Shoe and I went back long before Sylvia, and we were going ahead without her.

Ice carried his life's disappointments openly. He failed at trying to crank up a career in music and he resigned himself to stick with the first real job he found, working for the City and County. He had aged more than either Shoe or I, and that said a lot because I thought more and more like a has-been every day. When I mentioned that to Ice, he said, "If you're a has-been, then I'm a never-was."

We ran out of new things to talk about the same time I accepted that I was drunk. I tuned out their off-color puns and repetitive slurs against the economy. I prepared myself to call it a night.

Three women our age walked in the club. They quickly scouted the situation, talked among themselves and then headed in our direction. They knew us, we knew them and they had no problem sitting with us for a drink.

Isabel Scutti, Janey Martinez and Molly Gallagher were at the tail end of a bar-hopping night similar to ours, although they had enough sense to designate Janey as the sober driver. Before long, all six of us were laughing at stories of the old times at North High and the craziness in our present lives. The good party vibe returned and I caught my second wind.

I hesitated on specifics about me but the women knew more than I expected, including my divorce, my residency in the back room of Sylvia's shop and my loose connection to Artie Baca's recent demise. Thankfully, no one wanted much in the way of explanations.

I did say a few things about Artie. I thought it was the least I could do. I spoke about his funeral, the cop visits his death had generated and the strange encounter with Linda and Raymond Olivas. That stirred up the trash talk. Artie had no allies at the table, and we dredged up several stories about him, and Linda, that cemented his rotten reputation. Some of the stories I'd never heard, others I knew too well.

"That all seems long ago," I said. "Like it happened to someone else. Someone who had a better idea of what to do with his life."

"We've become less than we expected but more than we deserve," Isabel said. I remembered she graduated third in the class.

Her light brown hair tumbled around her shoulders. She had worn it very short in school. Her mouth smiled at everything and everyone. Gray eyes lit up with her smiles.

"You're having a good time," I said. "Celebrating something?"

"It's summer vacation. That's enough. This is one of those nights when good things happen. Like running into you three. It's been way too long since we hooked up with anyone from North. We always liked you guys. Too bad we didn't hang out more."

"Wish I'd known that back then," I said. "I had a serious crush on you. Thought you were out of my league."

"What a bunch of bull. Same old Gus. But I did like you. You were smart. Lazy, but smart."

"That's what my counselor said, too. At least about the lazy part."

She laughed and I moved my chair closer.

"How's the teaching job? You been at it for a while."

"I love the kids. You'd be surprised . . . well, maybe you wouldn't. I know teachers who don't even like their students. Don't know the families or their neighborhoods. No clue to what is going on in their kids' lives. Too many teachers are simply putting in their time for the pension."

"I had plenty of teachers like that. They kill school for a kid."

"So true. It's not all the teachers' fault. The families have to help, be involved. But the biggest thing is that the administration and bureaucracy freeze out creativity. At least, they try to. CSAP rules."

"What?"

"The Colorado Student Assessment Program. In some schools, that's all that counts. How the students do on those goddammed tests. Many of us plug along doing what we can. We spend our own money for supplies, set up special times for the parents, visit their homes. We never have time for ourselves. We battle principals and other teachers. I . . . God. I'm starting to sound like a union meeting. Old and dreary. I want to have fun. You want to have fun, don't you, Gus?"

"That's an invitation I'll never refuse. There's nothing old or dreary about you. I know dreary. I live it. You're not any way close."

She smiled like the sun coming up over the Eastern plains.

"Molly's got some pot in the car," she said. "Want a toke?"

"I thought you were a good Italian Catholic girl."

"I am. That's why I'm offering to share."

We left but no one noticed. Shoe and Ice were on their own, and doing well.

Isabel scurried out the back door when the sun popped through the window and warmed my cot and our naked bodies. I was embarrassed for her, leaving through the alley without breakfast, not so much as a kiss goodbye. I tried small talk, but we were caught up in morning-after awkwardness and she didn't want to talk with anyone, especially me. Her hangover was worse than mine. The night before, I traded Ice and Shoe for Isabel. More correctly, Shoe and Ice moved on when they realized that Isabel and I were going to be an item, at least for a few hours.

I dealt with my hangover with water and coffee and a few old doughnuts I had lying around, but mid-morning Reese and Robbins interrupted my convalescence, and it wasn't pleasant.

The two cops accused, threatened and mocked me. They were upbeat, gloating almost. I, on the other hand, could barely stay awake. I had a hell of a time keeping down the three-in-the-morning burritos Isabel and I scarfed after the clubs closed.

"We know you and Artie Baca were working together. That's what the check was supposed to be for." Crew-cut, tobacco-smelling Reese talked at me, not waiting for a response. "Linda Baca said she thought it was very weird that you would have had any business with her husband. It had to be something shady because she didn't know about it, and she knew everything he did, business-wise. Everything that was on the up-and-up."

"She said he left all that behind, years ago," Robbins chimed in. "You must have had something on him to get him to go along with you again." He came off surly, as rude as his older partner. I wondered what happened to good-cop, bad-cop. They were both offensive that morning.

"She said that?" I managed to say. "Why would she say such a thing?"

Robbins grunted. "Yeah, asshole, she said that. She told us how you and Baca were wannabe gangsters back when you were punks. She talked about the low-end B and E's you never got popped for, how your partnership ended when you finally got busted. We checked your record, a real cheap charge. Both of you walked away with nothing serious in your files. Linda says that was Artie's turning point. Apparently not for you, right, Gus?"

"I don't know what the hell you're talking about."

That was true. Right then nothing made sense, and it had as much to do with the shots of tequila from the night before as with my normal state of confusion.

Robbins glared at me like he was a wounded animal, and then he moved right up in my face. "Asshole," he seemed to like that word. "You're the one who knocked off Artie Baca. I know it, my partner knows it, and we're going to bust your ass, asshole." The smooth-looking, always professional policeman had a limited vocabulary.

"You go to public school, Robbins?" I asked.

He looked like he could explode. I shrugged. "I don't know why I said that."

He slapped me across the cheek and any other day I wouldn't have noticed but that day had a lot of wackiness built in. My face felt like someone had used a hot iron to wake me up, and my nose still ached from Jerome's punch, not to mention the beating Lorenzo's thugs gave me, so maybe I overreacted. Truth be told, it wasn't the pain or bruising or lumps that caused me to lunge at Robbins. I had enough of feeling like everybody's easy target. I charged Robbins but before I could throw a punch, Reese grabbed me by the armpits and lifted me off his partner. He wound up his delivery like a cartoon relief pitcher and slugged my gut. I doubled over. He threw me across the room into the wall. Robbins moved toward me and I prepared for another smackdown.

I held up my hands and tried to wave him back. He hesitated. I tasted sour burritos, gagged at the back of my throat, felt a wave of nausea and lost my doughnuts and burritos on the dusty floor of Sylvia's Superb Shoppe. Robbins stopped in his tracks. Specks of brown vomit dotted his black shoes.

"You pig. Look at the mess, you dumb piece of shit."

I mumbled and stumbled around the room, waiting for the cuffs and the ride downtown. I imagined the charges I might face—assaulting an officer, disrespecting an officer, grossing out an officer.

They didn't make the move. They made noises, for sure, smoke and fury without action. They shouted they were watching me and I was going down. An attack of hiccups seized me, but I managed to wave at the two cops when they escaped from the foul-smelling shop.

Eventually I cleaned up the shop and myself. Then I called Jerome. I had a hard time spitting it out, and he didn't act like he wanted to waste any time with me, but finally I said, "I need your help, Jerome."

"You got some balls, Gus. My nose still hurts."

"I thought you were over that."

"Think again."

"I have to talk to someone about all that's been happening. I don't understand it. Maybe you will. We've been friends too long, Jerome."

He ragged me for several minutes. I cringed, but stated my case and argued that he was the only person I could turn to for advice. Couldn't he see how I made the mistake of not trusting him? What would he have done?

He finally came around. "I kind of understand. I might have screwed up the same way, given the circumstances."

That's what I hoped for—we were dropped from the same mold and sooner or later Jerome had to see it. Two beans in a pod—that was Jerome and me.

"What happened to your business? Not that long ago this place was packed." There were few other customers. Jerome and I were the only ones sitting in the patio.

His nose looked bad—bloated, red and bruised. I didn't mention it.

"A new shop just opened up, on Tejon. It cut into my base, big time," he said. "That's the way it goes. Up one day, down the next.

People want to try out the newest thing, and that place offers what they call Cuban coffee and Cuban sandwiches. There's so many new coffee shops on the North Side we're killing ourselves. I'm competing with Cuban and Mexican and European and old-fashioned and cutesy and who knows what else. I don't sleep much, and it's not from sampling my product. I'm hoping that when the newness wears off, my regulars will come back."

The magazines Jerome laid out for his customers were full of stories, how all the experts were saying that we had finally bottomed out, but it sure didn't look like it from where I sat. New businesses had to be flukes, aberrations, freaks of nature. They couldn't all endure, and Jerome might become a casualty.

"You'll survive," I said despite my doubts. "You always have."

"Maybe." He sipped on his espresso and snarled his words. "What's bothering you now? Why the rush to talk?"

"The cops, Reese and Robbins, dropped by, it got ugly. They tossed me around. I had to defend myself, commit the crime of self-defense. But the strange thing is that they didn't do anything about it. Nothing serious, I mean."

That caught his attention. He put down his coffee.

"They think I had something to do with Artie's murder. They keep accusing me but they don't take me downtown, they just walk away. It's like they want me to twist in the air, know what I mean? Like they're playing a game, but what's the payoff? It's bugging the hell out of me. What's going on?"

"I didn't think any cop would ever pass up a chance to arrest you. It doesn't take much to get pinched for assaulting an officer, resisting arrest, all that bullshit. You're a lucky guy, Gus."

"People keep saying that and I repeat—I don't feel lucky. I feel used, set-up, but I don't know for what."

He took his time answering. He watched a guy with thin graying hair, dressed in sweat pants and a sweatshirt, pick up his order at the counter. A blond woman also in workout clothes waited at the door, a few feet from where we sat. She winked at Jerome.

"Yeah, could be a set-up," he said. "I once got popped for a warehouse break-in but it took the police weeks to make the pinch.

They tailed me everywhere I went. Talked to all my friends. Visited me several times, letting me know that they knew all about me. They spooked me, serious. When the arrest finally went down, I was relieved in a way. I got so nervous that I hustled the warehouse stuff too early—electronics, remote controls, DVDs, that kind of junk. It was stupid, I wasn't ready but I choked. They didn't have enough on me until then. It took some fancy and expensive legal work to get me out of that one."

"The difference between you and me is that I didn't do anything, so this game they're playing won't do them any good. Meanwhile, I'm getting squeezed for no reason. That damn Baca."

"If what you told me about Carne Ortiz is true, that's your way out. Give him up to the cops." He couldn't even finish that sentence with a straight face.

"Give him up to the cops. Right. Not going to happen. I can't do more than I already have, not if I want to stay alive. I've led them to Ortiz when he beat me up. I've put out the word I was looking for his sister and asking about her link to Artie. I've done everything but draw a map for the two police cowboys, but they won't move off of me."

"Then you got to do something else."

"Like what?"

"You think I know? I've never been a snitch, so this is new territory for me."

"I ain't a snitch. I need to protect myself. I got to come up with something. I can't sit back and let the cops railroad me."

He stood up. "Your odds are like slim to none. No one beats the cops at their own hustle. Least, no one I've known for a long time. Let me think about it. Come around tonight, over to my house. Maybe we can put something together." He turned away, then turned back. "I don't know why I'm doing this. I shouldn't be. Laters."

"Yeah, whatever. I'll see you tonight. Thanks."

He walked away. I had to trust him, what else could I do?

15

Corrine stopped by that afternoon. "I heard you picked up Isabel Scutti." First words out of her mouth. "She's way out of your league, brother. How'd you pull it off?" Good old Corrine, never missed an opportunity to drive the knife deeper.

"My charm, what else? When did you hear about Isabel? What happened to my privacy?"

"You must have got her drunk. One thing led to another, eh? She had that reputation in school. There was a good story behind why everyone called her 'Three Beers.'"

Three shots of Patrón Silver worked, too, but Corrine didn't need to know all the details.

"I'm glad to see you, too, Corrine. What's new?"

She looked out the windows of the shop. She sniffed and touched the front door, feeling for dust.

"Smells like Lysol in here. You been cleaning up?"

"Yeah, figured it was time to at least mop the floor. Didn't you notice?"

She eyed the floor. "Hard to tell the difference. You must have been bored."

"I'm never bored, believe me. There's plenty going on in my life. But what I asked was, what's new with you? What do I owe this visit to? Somebody else steal Panchito?"

"No, nothing like that. I had to get out of the house. I've been feeling . . . I don't know what . . . nervous about something. Like something's going to happen, and it won't be good. I get these feelings every once in a while."

"Yeah, and most of the time nothing happens. What could go bad with you? All the weird shit is happening to me, as usual."

"I don't know what it is. Like someone's watching me, but I haven't seen anyone unusual hanging around the house or anything like that." She craned her neck to look up and down the street.

"Maybe it's the cops. The doughnut squad's hassling me about Artie. They were here earlier today and they stunk up the place so bad I cleaned up, as you noticed. They might have someone watching you, hoping that you lead them to the murder weapon so they can finally arrest me. That's probably what it is. Just the cops."

"That might be it, I guess. If I see them I'll tell them you confessed. That should get them to leave me alone. You think?"

"You're funny, Corrine. Funny like sitting on a cactus."

Corrine didn't laugh or smile or act in any way like she heard my flat joke. "This feeling of yours, it really has you worried?" I asked.

"I said that, didn't I?"

"What do you want to do about it? I could stay with you for a few days. Maybe I'll see something or someone."

Normally she shot down a suggestion like that without any second thoughts. Corrine never needed a bodyguard or chaperone. She could be flighty, sure, but never uptight defensive. This time, though, she weighed my offer.

"Thanks, Gus. It's all right. Imagining stuff—I must be getting old or something. You're the one who should worry. At least I don't have any gangsters after me."

She left a few minutes later and when she did, she made sure to survey the street before she walked out the door. She turned and waved at me with a smile that looked as fake as her hair color.

Jerome's house sat on a hill near the Willis Case golf course, not too far from I-70. The view offered the city skyline in one direction and the mountains in the other, each framed by the noisy, always busy freeway. He inherited the creaking, leaking Victorian house from an aunt who favored him over his brother and sister, for a reason he never explained to me. When he had the money he did what he could to fix up the house. He kept at least one project going at all times—kitchen remodeling, plumbing repair, land-scaping—and the house never looked finished. Pallets of bricks, cans of paint and rolls of wire or sod cluttered the yard. Boxes of tile, shelving and windowpanes sat in corners and hallways. His purchases exceeded the time he had to devote to rehab chores, but he figured he would buy all that he could while he had the money. He worked with the materials on hand, seldom completely ending one job before he started another. He was good with his hands and had a designer's eye. The house gradually came together and its disheveled, under-construction appearance looked better than the way I remembered it when Jerome first moved in.

I sat on his couch. I held a dark Dos Equis. He sipped on a full glass of red wine.

"That's new." I pointed at a massive painting of blue and gray naked bodies.

Several paintings hung on his walls, all by Latino artists but nothing typically "Latino." He preferred what he called "the more modern," odd shapes with bright colors, or highly stylized figures like the bare asses, tits and other body parts hanging on his living room wall.

"Who did it?"

"Young lady named Carla Martínez. I saw it at CHAC. One of those First Friday things. The gallery was packed, like it always is for that night. Quite a street party. I saw the artist standing next to this piece." He pointed his wine at the painting. "Pretty thing. I didn't know she was the artist, not until we talked for a few minutes, which was hard to do in the crowd. She's doing a series, calling them her Blue and Gray Forms. This is #2."

I looked again at the painting but I didn't like it. I guessed it was technically all right, and the colors mixed well, but the nudity did nothing for me. I kept my opinion to myself.

"I'm going to be one of her models for #3." He added that bit too carelessly.

"Naked?"

"Yeah, what else? That's kind of the idea, Gus."

"You dog."

"It's not what you think." His smile said otherwise.

"Right. You're dropping your pants for art's sake. I like it, that's good. With all your crying about the economy, you must have bucks to afford that painting."

He bobbed his head left and right—maybe yes, maybe no.

"I manage. I always have several irons in the fire. The painting? Carla lent it to me after her exhibit closed. I may buy it, don't know yet. We're working on the details."

My man, Jerome. Whatever he said could have a double meaning, at least to a guy like me who read something into everything I saw or heard. Given Jerome's history I had no problem taking Jerome's words in their most sinister or devious meaning. His "other irons" had to be illegal. "Working out the details" with the artist meant he was hitting that. Sex and art, always a nice combination. Or he could mean nothing at all except the obvious, but that's never where my head went concerning Jerome.

"Any ideas for me regarding my situation with the cops?"

"A few. It may be in your best interest to meet with the two . . . "

A noise in the back yard—a squeaky gate—made him stand and peer through one of his windows, then we both rushed to the back kitchen. We looked at one another. He shook his head, and then reached up to open a cupboard door. I never learned what he hoped to find. The back door burst open. I heard splintering wood and the tinkle of broken glass. Four men carrying guns crashed through the kitchen door.

Jerome moved as fast as I have ever seen him move. He ran, more like rolled, to the closest corner where he picked up a hammer from a bucket of tools, but one of the gunmen knocked him down with the butt of what looked like an AK-47. A man with silver rings on his fingers pushed me into a wall and pressed a gun against my forehead.

The four men breathed deep and hard. They moved their weapons back and forth and I could see sweat on their faces. They forced Jerome and me to our knees. They pointed their guns at us but did not say anything.

Lorenzo Ortiz eased the battered door out of his way and walked into Jerome's house.

"Look what we got here. Gus and his best pal. It's a bad night for Gus' friends." He laughed his hyena laugh.

"Leave Jerome out of this. He's got nothing to do with your sister or Baca."

Ortiz ignored me.

He shouted orders in Spanish. "Let's go. Get them to the truck. It's your ass if we get caught. Let's go."

The man with silver rings stretched duct tape across my mouth and dropped a hood over my head. He jerked me to my feet, wrenched my hands behind my back and secured them with plastic restraints. He pushed me out of the house and down the back yard walkway. The alley gate squeaked when it swung open. Jerome grunted as he struggled and someone hit him.

Two of the men picked me up and tossed me into the bed of a pickup truck. They draped a canvas tarp over Jerome and me, and the truck moved. Ortiz had grabbed me again. My jaw still cramped from the last time his men stuck duct tape on me, my body still ached from the beating. What did this guy want?

About every five minutes I felt the barrel of a gun jab my ribs.

16

I thought we were in the back of the truck for hours, but that came from my thumping heart and nauseous stomach. Jerome and I were dead, there was no doubt. Ortiz had snatched me twice, the first time to warn me off and this second time to carry out the threat. It had to be, and yet I didn't know what it was that Ortiz thought I'd done that deserved my execution. But the gangster didn't need a rational excuse, did he? He was a killer, a stone-cold murderer. That was what I tried to clue the cops to. Was I paying the price for being half-in, half-out with the police? I lay in the back of that shaking, noisy truck bed, trussed up like a Thanksgiving turkey ready for carving. I understood that I should have gone straight up to Reese and Robbins, but it was too late.

Ortiz must have concluded that I was too much of a loose cannon, that I knew too much about his blackmailing Artie, and that he was more secure if I was out of the way, no matter how insignificant I might be to the big picture. He probably believed he had revealed too much during our cozy conversation in his car.

My lungs couldn't heave in enough air. I choked and gasped. The hood stuck to my skin, my sweat soaked the rough cloth, and I felt dizzy, weak. I bounced with each rut in the road and occasionally I hit Jerome, or he smashed into me. The men around us in the pickup bed laughed and told jokes about us that I didn't think were funny. I wanted the truck to stop, but stopping meant the end, in more ways than one. I cursed Artie Baca and the day he dragged me back into his life.

The truck slowed down until it idled in place. I heard a loud grating noise—chains clanging across concrete. Then I heard what sounded like a large metal garage door opening and shutting. The truck moved ahead for a few seconds before it thudded to a stop.

Jerome and I were pushed out of the bed and onto a concrete floor. The hoods came off. We were in a huge building. I guessed that it was empty but I couldn't say for sure.

I smelled oil, gasoline and rubber. A circle of light surrounded us, but I could see only a dim gray illumination from the roof. The rest was darkness.

Lorenzo Ortiz appeared and whispered to one of his men, who then rushed into the dark. Ortiz looked freaky—shiny skin in ghostly light and eyes that wouldn't stop moving. We all waited for a few minutes. Ortiz's sick laugh broke the silence a couple of times. No one said anything. Ortiz's men cradled their weapons or smoked cigarettes.

The man returned, followed by Corrine and Isabel. Both were tied up like Jerome and me with tape across their faces. Another man with another gun trailed the women. I jerked and struggled but it did no good. When I saw the fear in Isabel's eyes and the blood dripping from Corrine's mouth I finally accepted the dangerous reach of my gamble with Ortiz. Artie's mess, the two slow but determined cops and the guy who broke into my room behind Sylvia's shop—the images swirled together into a pounding headache, a crazy dream except that I was wide awake. Whatever I'd tried to do, whatever idiocy I had concocted in my confused brain to nail Ortiz for Artie's killing, had failed miserably. I wasn't the only one who would pay for my screw-up.

Lorenzo Ortiz stood in front of Jerome and me. He held a pistol, a small handgun that was almost buried in his large right hand.

"I have a story for you, Gus, you and your amigo. Let me see if I can tell it right." He looked like he was enjoying himself. "Friends of mine. No. Ex-friends. Anyhow, these guys I know did a really terrible thing a while back. Maybe you heard about it? The cabrones who raided the basilica in the capital, and stole the sacred tilma. You know about that, right? Of course you do."

Unsmiling, he looked around at his men. They stared back at him, or us, also without smiles, without any expression.

"My men heard about that savage act, that disgraceful event, and they lost all respect for the organization, for the pendejos at the top and I can't say they're wrong, can I? I thought I knew the fools that run the club, but you never really know anybody, not really, verdad? I was shocked and surprised when I heard about it, like my men. But what can we do? We're only soldiers, not generals. The bosses decided they were going to steal from La Virgen de Guadalupe, and we had to go along. Until today, Gus. That's where you come in."

I shook my head and tried to make a face that said I didn't know what the hell he was talking about, but it didn't have any noticeable effect.

"These stupid bosses decide—on their own again, no input from me—they decide that they have to move the merchandise out of Mexico as quickly as they can. It's way too hot to have around, not when every cop in the world is looking for it, not when there are professionals prowling around Mexico digging hard to find it. The country is overrun with FBI and CIA and cops from countries like Spain and Italy. Even the damn pope has men on the streets. Does it take a genius to know that's what would happen? How smart do you have to be to know that there will be incredible heat when you rip off La Virgen?"

Lorenzo sweated across his forehead. He wiped his face with his left hand while he thought about his words.

"The bosses," he said, "being the brains they are, tell me that I have to watch out for the sacred thing, that I have to put my operation and my men at risk for something I had no say about. Can you fucking believe that bullshit?" Spit sprayed my face as his right fist, still holding the gun, slammed against the palm of his left hand. "They deliver the thing to me, and I have to watch it. I have to babysit a blanket like I got nothing else to do, like I don't have every Denver cop sniffing around every damn day." Again his words exploded and ricocheted around the building. "Can you fucking believe it?"

The Butcher had lost his mind. His story had nothing to do with me, and it certainly had nothing to do with Corrine, Isabel and Jerome. Yet, there we all were, waiting like cattle for the slaughter and at the mercy of a crazy man who, for some reason, wanted me to know that he didn't like the guys he worked for.

He ripped the duct tape from my mouth. I thought he tore off my lips. He did open a scab on my cheek, left over from the first beating his men gave me. Blood trickled down my chin. I took it as a sign that he wanted me to say something.

"What's any of that got to do with us? Why are we here? What do you want? Let the others go."

He pointed the gun at my face and I shut up.

"I'm giving you a big break, Gus. Your lucky day. You get the chance to be famous, even notorious. All you have to do is steal the tilma here in Denver and you and your friends are free."

My mouth must have dropped open because he gave me another one of his strange-sounding laughs.

"It's simple, Gus. You steal the blanket, make it look real good. I tell the idiots I work for that it's been taken, then, when no one's looking, you give it back to me. The bosses are pissed, but they have to think things through, which buys me time, then they almost certainly come after me for losing the thing, but by then I've sold it to the pope or anyone else who wants it, for more money than you can imagine, and I get out of this damn country, and away to where no one will ever find me, not even the pinche bosses."

His insane plan would never work but how do you argue logic with a crazy man? I said things like "You can't be serious," or "I don't know how to do what you want," or "Why don't you just take it yourself when you get your hands on it?"

He finally responded to the last question. "They're not really giving it to me, Gus. That's the problem, güey. They've sent it up here to the States, and I got to use my men to watch it, but it's under the guard of a hand-picked crew from Mexico City. They won't have it out of their sight. We're just sort of guarding the guards, entiendes? We could shoot them all, but that's messy, and I'd lose some of my best men. For sure I'd be a marked man and I wouldn't have the time I need to make my deal. Blaming the rip-off on you gives me the time I need."

He nodded his head, agreeing with his own brilliance. A few of his men also nodded their heads—they were all in, counting on the Butcher to make a play that even in their dulled and demented minds they must have realized had little chance.

Ortiz finished his rap. "Those psychos who are escorting the tilma are way on the edge, man, I know. I used to hang around with them. Anyhow, the key thing is that you give me time, Gus. Yeah, this is your big chance."

He looked very pleased with himself. His eyes glowed with excitement, or drugs, or both. His smile flashed in the spotlight like the rhinestones on the cheap jewelry back in Sylvia's shop. His irksome laugh bounced around the building. We became the audience for his performance. The perfect score finally landed in his lap, so he thought, and if it worked the way his twisted brain thought it would work, he wouldn't risk anything more than the sorry life of a loser who insisted on getting involved with him, and a couple of the loser's friends and relatives.

"That crew from Mexico City. You called them hand-picked. They'll make a quick end to anything I might try. I'll be dead, and the botched robbery will make the bosses suspicious. They'll tie you to it."

"No, señor. They don't think that quick. They'll need to analyze, take their time like they do with everything. Worse than old ladies. My idea is a good one. Up to you to make it happen."

I insisted and kept on rolling out the reasons why his plan was doomed to failure until he shut me up by knocking my head with his gun.

"You're going to do it, Gus. No argument. If you don't, then your sister and girlfriend get to spend a long night with my men, and I can promise you that by morning their wish to be dead will be granted. It's that simple. You get your hands on the tilma and you all walk away. I'll be out of here and won't care about you and your friends. Or you die trying. Either way, my problems with you are solved."

He motioned to his men and they scurried away into the darkness. He lit a cigarette.

"I'll come back in the morning, Gus. We'll talk about the details. You all stay here for the night, get some rest. Manuel, one of my best guys, will watch over you. He'll be around even if you don't see him. Give it some thought, Gus. You're going to need damn good preparation to rip off the tilma from the Mexico City boys. Those chilangos are cabrones, but they know how to keep something safe. You're going to be a busy man tomorrow." He walked out of the light.

The four of us huddled together. I was the only one without tape on my mouth so we couldn't talk. We made our way to the wall, slumped against the concrete and stared at nothing. Manuel appeared with bottles of water and bags of potato chips. He was an older guy with at least ten years on the other thugs. His eyelids hung heavy over his eyeballs. I recognized the machete tattoo from the night at the restaurant when Lorenzo's men beat me up. Manuel seemed to enjoy the workout that night.

He removed the tape from the other three, freed our wrists, told us to drink the water, and then a real surprising thing happened. He gave Jerome a big hug. They patted one another on the back, and then I knew who gave Misti Ortiz's phone number to Jerome. Jerome had friends everywhere and one of them turned out to be the Butcher's right hand guy.

Manuel smiled at Corrine, who half-heartedly smiled back, but they shied away from each other like there was an invisible wall between them. Corrine had friends, and ex-friends, everywhere, too, and she and Manuel must have had a history.

Manuel stepped back into the darkness and let us talk.

They gave me hell, of course. Corrine started, Jerome continued and Isabel—innocent, unaware and scared—ripped into me like a drunken barber with a rusty pair of scissors.

I didn't blame them. Their lives were seriously at risk and it was entirely my fault, in ways they couldn't even guess.

The blood around Corrine's mouth had dried but her upper lip looked like an overripe plum—always a fighter. Jerome also had bruises and cuts and a smear of mud across his cheek, but the look in his eyes told me he was standing up well, still strong. Isabel was another story. The consequences of a one-night stand can be bad, even deadly, but it never crossed her mind that spending time with the class clown would result in her kidnapping and imprisonment. I wanted to tell her I was sorry and that I would make it right but the words wouldn't come out, mainly because I didn't believe them myself.

When the three finally stopped slamming me, a nervous silence fell on us. Guilt smothered me and most of it came from what I had done to Isabel. She'd walked into my mess of a life without any warnings. I guessed that Ortiz's men had jumped to a conclusion about her and me because of the one-night stand. Max or Sylvia as hostages made more sense, in terms of a connection to me. If we escaped alive I swore to myself to make it up to her. I had no idea how I could do that.

"Can't your friend help?" I asked Jerome. "He could get us out of here tonight."

Jerome shook his head. "He's not that good of a friend. We partnered up for a few gigs a couple of years ago. But those were different times."

"Corrine?" I said.

"Manuel's not a friend," she said. "I know him. That's it. I can't ask him for anything. We're probably lucky he doesn't shoot us all."

"Anyway," Jerome said, "there must be men outside, just in case. Ortiz wouldn't trust us to one man. Even if Manuel let us go, it wouldn't do any good. The rest of the gang would capture us again, or kill us, and Manuel, too."

"I figure Ortiz will send me and Jerome after the tilma," I said. "He'll keep Corrine and Isabel for security. We can't do anything unless we have some leverage. The only thing that could be is the tilma, or our own guns."

Jerome agreed. "Juan Diego's poncho is our only weapon. To make sure we get away with our lives, we have to use what Ortiz wants, against him." He looked at each one of us. "I don't know how we do it. It doesn't look good."

"No, it doesn't," Corrine said. "But you guys have to take care of business. We have to get some help. Maybe we can get word to someone when Ortiz sets everything in motion. That might be your chance."

"Maybe," I said. "But slim. We don't have phones, and they aren't going to leave us alone."

"Yeah, I don't think it'll go down that way," Jerome said. "We need something else, someone else to help us." He peered into the dark building and lowered his voice to a whisper. "Maybe from Ortiz's crew. We try to buy one off. These guys are always for sale to the highest bidder. They change teams like they throw away empty beer cans. They have no loyalty. You heard Ortiz talk about his bosses, his former running buddies. It's all about the money, that's what loyalty means to them."

I nodded. "We'll work on that angle, talk it up with whoever we end up with tomorrow. Even if Ortiz gets wind of what we're trying to do, so what? We don't have anything to lose."

We all thought about what I said. The women settled back against the wall.

"Ortiz is a lunatic," I said to Jerome.

"Tell me something I don't know."

"Yeah, he's crazy, but why drag us into this? This is a big deal, a life-changer for him. He's double-crossing his outfit, one of the biggest and most violent gangs in Mexico. He can't go back after this. He's risking everything."

"It's how he thinks. This job will set him up for life. There's a mountain of money to be made off the Virgin. He's betting everything on it. That's all that matters to him."

"Sure, sure. But why use us? We're not part of his gang. We could easily screw it up. Most likely we will. He knows that. Yet, here we are. We could sabotage the plan, make a run for it. Do almost anything except make it work for him. So, why us?"

Jerome thought for a few seconds. "It's what he said. He believes by using us he's one more step removed from the scrutiny of his boss. If it goes bad tomorrow, he can claim that we, the outsiders, planned the rip-off and died trying. Even if we succeed, he still lays the blame on us until he gets his pay-off, stalling the boss from looking at him too close, and then he disappears. We're his cover, Gus. I think it's as simple as that."

"He's going to have to use some of his men," I said. "He knows better than to leave it all up to you and me."

"That's right. Whoever those men are, they'll be thrown to the dogs along with us. Ortiz will say they're turncoats who climbed in bed with the two outlaws from Denver. When we're all dead, who's to say otherwise?"

That reality settled in and we quit talking. Manuel returned and secured our hands and taped our mouths again. We tried to sleep. Occasionally I heard a whimper from Isabel. Jerome actually snored for several minutes. Corrine twisted and turned, trying to find a comfortable position on the concrete, but with her hands tied together making her arch her back, it was useless and I knew she wouldn't sleep all night.

Neither would I.

17

Misti Ortiz showed up around three in the morning. Manuel stood nearby, his back to us, watching for any late night visitors. I knew it was Misti as soon as my eyes focused. The stark, gaunt face, not beautiful but something else, drew me into her world—lost, wounded—the almost boyish short black hair, the silver ring in her eyebrow, the eyes with a sad glow. Artie disregarded his wife and kids and nice home near Sloan's Lake once he looked into those eyes. But I wouldn't let myself forget that she was only fifteen.

She wore jeans, sneakers and a thin fleece jacket. She could have been a cheerleader on her way to the homecoming dance. She could have been a teenaged killer cleaning up her latest job.

She touched a ring-laden finger to her lips and motioned me to move away from Corrine, Isabel and Jerome. She snipped off the restraints. I rubbed my sore wrists.

She finally stood in front of me, but I didn't know what to say. I reminded myself that she tried to swindle Artie Baca. She used her obvious sexuality and too young body to extract money from my old pal. The way she played him freaked him out in such a major way that he lost all sense and believed that he could win the dangerous match. I didn't think I was any smarter than Artie, but I had an advantage since I wasn't about to let a fifteen-year-old girl use me. At least that's what I told myself would never happen. She loosened the tape around my mouth.

"You're Artie's friend. You tried to reach me after he was killed. Wanting to find out what happened to him?"

"Yeah . . . well, I know what happened to him. I'm not sure what I was trying to do, except that I thought I needed to talk with you. I was trying to find out more about why. I don't know, some-thing like that."

I couldn't tell her I tried to lead the cops to Lorenzo in my clumsy way. It seemed incredibly stupid when I stood in the early morning darkness of a deserted building, a prisoner of her crimi-nal brother, at the mercy of thugs and whatever she was—whore, blackmailer, killer?

"Maybe you were after Lorenzo? He must have been the one who killed Artie. His men brag about it."

Her talk made me nervous. It didn't seem the time or place to bring up the sordid mess between her, Artie and her brother.

"I'm not after anyone. That's why this is crazy. All of this . . . it makes no sense. Why would your brother want to drag us into this? What is he trying to do?"

Corrine stirred and mumbled incoherent words. Isabel turned on her side. Jerome watched us.

"No one understands why Lorenzo does what he does," Misti said. "I think half the time he doesn't know himself. He just acts. He's a simple man, with simple pleasures like causing pain, tor-menting people."

The way she said it convinced me she knew too many details of her brother's fondness for causing pain.

"But me, and my sister, my friends? We have nothing to offer him. There's nothing we can do for him."

"Like I said, it gives him pleasure to watch the pain of others. When he finds someone to target, he doesn't stop until the end, whatever he decides the end is. You made it to his list, and now he'll do whatever he wants with you. He'll do it because he can, and he doesn't think you can stop him. He doesn't care if you're killed, if everyone in this room is killed. It's the way he enjoys life." She stopped and looked around, remembering where she was and who might be listening. "Do you think you can do something? Can you finally stop him, Gus Corral?"

Before I could answer, she reached into a red leather purse and flashed a handgun. I shuddered, and for a second I thought I would pay for Artie's sins. I silently cursed that thousand dollar check again.

"This is all I can get you now," she said. "This extra gun will give you an advantage. The men outside think I'm here to bring them and Manuel some food and beer. I'm lucky they didn't search me. Too afraid of Lorenzo and what he might do if they disrespected his sister." The ugly Ortiz laugh escaped from her mouth. "Tomorrow, Manuel will do what he can. Follow his lead. If you don't get away, Lorenzo will kill all of you once you take the tilma. If you get a chance, you have to kill Lorenzo."

I stammered, "How? What . . . ?"

She shook her head to silence me. She rubbed her hands down the front of her jacket, wiping away the deadly words she had said against her brother.

"I hope to see you again, but the odds are that I won't." The coldness of her words matched the dead air in the warehouse. "Cuídate. Be careful. Any mistake and you're dead," then she turned away into the dark building.

I stuffed the gun in the waistband of my pants. Manuel walked over to me.

"Tomorrow," he said in a whisper, "you either escape or you die. Those are the only two things that can happen, and we both know which one is more likely. When we get to where the tilma is hidden, you have to make your move quick. You'll know it's happening because I'll start shooting. Warn your friends tonight. Get them ready."

"Why? What's in this for you?"

He snapped open a golden lighter and methodically lit a cigarette.

"I can't go along with stealing from La Virgen," he said. "He hecho algunos desmadres. I'm no saint. But I can't do this, what Ortiz is asking. It goes against everything I still believe. If I get my hands on the tilma, I'm returning it to Mexico City. I'll put it back where it belongs."

The hard set of his face loosened. His jaw bone relaxed.

"You don't think we'll make it," I said. "Is it worth it?"

"None of us are worth it, like you say. But I'll do what I have to do." He threw away his smoke. "Son los años. I'm getting too old.

All my true friends are dead, or never going to leave prison. I've become expendable. Lorenzo expects me to get killed tomorrow. I'm not going to go out the way he thinks." He turned to walk away. I grabbed his shoulder. He jerked and grabbed my hand.

"Easy," I said. "I have to ask. Why is Misti doing this? Her own brother?"

He let go of my hand. "Her brother, yeah. Y también, her pimp. Since she was twelve. Using her to trap men, and then forcing them to pay money. So young, but she's too old, también. Old and tired."

Jerome moved in the background. He mumbled a few grunts to let us know he was awake. He eagerly accepted the second gun after I explained the visit from Misti and Manuel's part in the plan.

"At least we have a chance now," he said when I removed the tape from his face. "Why'd they do that, Gus? Why help us? That girl doesn't even know us."

Corrine and Isabel were awake, listening to us. I removed the tapes from their mouths.

"Manuel has his own reasons. Misti? It's not so much that she's helping us," I said. "She's trying to get away from her brother, get him killed really. She's finally had enough."

"She wants you and Jerome to do her dirty work." That was Corrine. "You'd think she'd want to pull the trigger herself. She must be afraid of him."

"Whatever she's been through, she's just a kid, a young girl," Isabel said. "Her brother is a monster. She's doing the only thing she can think of." I agreed. Misti Ortiz lived in a world I could never understand or accept. She had survived terrible things that had forever warped her, but she was a kid. A very dangerous, twisted kid.

18

Morning arrived like a kick in the head. Manuel and his men ran into the building, shouting, cursing. They rousted us from the concrete, hustled us into a small room and before we were fully awake we were instructed on our simple task: steal the Blessed Virgin's image from heavily armed, cold-blooded killers. Lorenzo Ortiz was nowhere in sight.

"There will be four guards and they won't be expecting any trouble—not from us for sure," Manuel said. He took his time, giving details that had double meaning for those of us who intended to use the heist as the cover for our escape.

Salvador, a short muscular man with a bald head and a thick mustache, stood in a corner, listening to Manuel. Tattoos covered his Popeye arms and what I could see of his neck.

"We're going to the basement of a downtown hotel, the Majestic. The jefes have arranged for a sale to a sinvergüenza from California, a collector who thinks that the tilma will look good surrounded by his Nazi flags and Hitler photographs."

"You're kidding," Jerome said.

"He's got the money and the bosses think it's a better idea to sell to him than to the pope. Too risky with el Papa."

"This is sick," I said.

Manuel didn't disagree.

"You two and Salvador and me will go through the hotel's parking garage to the basement. The buyer is staying in the hotel. He wants to view the merchandise, up close, so the tilma is only minutes from him. It's been there for a few days but he doesn't know it. Lorenzo runs the kitchen in the hotel. I mean, he has men that run it, so he's got an in. He arranged for the hotel room, a ride from the airport, todo. We're supposed to get there around ten this morning. The buyer shows up at ten-thirty, but by then it will be over. If things work out the way Lorenzo wants them to, the Mexico City guys will be dead, the tilma will be gone and the buyer will be left holding the bag since the cops will be alerted to check out the basement at the same time that the buyer is supposed to show up."

"What if it doesn't work? What if we're the dead ones? The collector gets what he bargained for? How does that make Lorenzo happy?"

Manuel and Salvador grinned at my questions.

"If it all goes to hell," Manuel said, "Lorenzo is still covered. The sale goes through, Lorenzo gets his cut and you guys are labeled 'home-grown terrorists' killed in a suicidal attack on the hotel. Since you'll be dead in the hotel basement, who's to say otherwise? Lorenzo can arrange for it to look like all of us followed orders from almost any group of locos anywhere in the world. If his plan works and by some miracle we escape with the holy image, he ends up with the tilma and can sell it himself to the buyer, or to anyone he wants—for the price he wants to set, and he doesn't have to split it with anyone."

Jerome shook his head. "We're dead men either way. As soon as the shooting starts the cops will bust into that basement, not to mention the hotel security. The Mexico City guys shoot us, or the cops take us out, or Lorenzo finishes what he started." He looked Manuel square in the eyes. "Or you."

Manuel grinned again.

Jerome finished with, "We have no reason to do this."

"You understand that Lorenzo will be holding the two women?" Manuel asked. "That's your reason, hombre. At least it's Gus' reason. Doing what Lorenzo wants is the only chance you have of making it out of here alive."

He gripped his handgun just in case Jerome missed his message. I forced myself to believe that Manuel and Jerome were playing hard ass with each other for the benefit of Salvador and the reports that he had to be sending to Lorenzo at least every hour.

"Yeah, I know what we have to do," Jerome said. "Don't worry about that."

"When we get to the basement, we'll be about ten minutes early," Manuel said. "We park on the lowest level, walk through the parking lot, take the freight elevator to the sub-basement and walk down a hallway to storage rooms filled with hotel scrap. Old pictures, furniture, beds, that kind of junk. We knock on the middle door, the boys inside let us in. They'll be watchful but not too excited. They know we're supposed to be there. Immediately we get it done. We start blasting, duck for cover and hope we survive. Those guys have to go down in a few seconds or it's over."

Jerome and I nodded.

"The tilma's in a fancy metal chest, protected from everything, including bullets. As soon as we can, we grab the chest, me and Salvador, and we run like hell to the stairs, we can't wait for the elevator. You guys cover us from behind. We run up to our ride in the parking lot. The tilma doesn't weigh anything at all but the chest is heavy. Salvador and I can handle it. We jump in the van and drive three blocks, where we ditch it and transfer the chest to Lorenzo. Then the four of us split up and walk away, like nothing is going on. Four guys who don't know each other walking around downtown Denver. You two wait for the women to show up at Jerome's house."

No way, I thought, for the hundredth time. But we had no choice.

Our training ended as abruptly as it started. Lorenzo's crew marched Corrine and Isabel through a side door, then they herded Jerome and me into a windowless van. Someone handed us Styrofoam cups with strong black coffee. We didn't get a chance to say goodbye or good luck. Everything happened too fast, with too much of a blur for me to get my bearings.

Jerome and I didn't talk during the ride. Salvador clogged the air in the van with cigarette smoke. I was hungry and exhausted but the coffee did make me feel better. Jerome drank his quietly without comment. He had to be thinking about his own coffee business a thousand miles, and years, away.

For a hot minute I considered using the gun Misti Ortiz gave me to disarm Salvador and take over the van. But the Mexican cradled an old-fashioned shotgun with a short handle. He never took his eyes off Jerome and me. He occasionally lifted his double-barreled weapon in our direction. I didn't have to be an Einstein to see that he wanted any excuse to use it on us. We didn't have a chance in the van.

I did not expect any of us, Corrine, Isabel, Jerome or me, to be alive at the end of the day.

19

I convinced myself that I had to get the drop on Manuel and Salvador before we confronted the Mexico City guns. That much I knew for sure. After that, it got a bit hazy. I guessed that for Salvador's benefit, Manuel intended to go through the motions of Lorenzo's plan and pass guns to Jerome and me just before we entered the storage room. I also figured that after the shootout, assuming we were still alive, Salvador would finish us off like Lorenzo must have ordered.

The Majestic rose for nineteen stories from the Sixteenth Street Mall. Manuel waited for traffic to clear, then he drove into an entrance to the parking lot off of Lawrence. We quickly descended through the parking levels. We jerked around tight corners on the hard-curving ramp until the van slowed and stopped near a space with an orange cone. Manuel left the van, moved the cone, jumped back in the driver's seat, then parked.

Manuel took the lead across the gray parking lot. He carried a canvas shopping bag with a yellow smiley face logo. Salvador waited for Jerome and me to get in line behind Manuel, then he followed us.

"I thought it'd be cooler down here," I said to Jerome. He grunted.

In the dim light the lot looked half-full but I didn't see other people. Manuel walked briskly to the freight elevator doors, almost running.

"Follow me," he said. "Don't forget why we're here, especially when the shooting starts. Stay on point. It's your only chance of walking out of here today."

Salvador pounded his palm against the stock of his shotgun. Drops of sweat fell from his nose.

Our footsteps echoed from car to car. Our shoes scraped on the concrete floor. I touched the handle of my gun hanging under my shirt. The solid metal reassured me, but only for a second.

We stepped into the roomy but grimy elevator, each one of us separated from the others, wary and watchful. Manuel punched the SB button and the elevator moved slow and with a lot of noise. I jumped at a loud screech from the top of the elevator. Jerome smiled. Manuel smiled back. They appeared relaxed, as if they'd been born to end up in that parking lot, that elevator, that day.

The elevator ground to a stop and opened onto a narrow hallway bathed in garish white from flickering light bulbs. Manuel headed for the middle door—a gray piece of metal with a small rectangular window protected by wire mesh. Salvador stayed behind us, still gripping his shotgun.

Manuel reached into his bag and took out a pistol. He aimed it in my direction. I jerked my hidden gun from my pants but then I froze in place. Manuel squeezed the trigger and I fell to my knees. Salvador crumpled at my feet. Blood gushed from his tattooed throat. He gurgled and thrashed on the floor. My pant cuffs soaked up his blood.

The door jerked open and the smooth dark face of a young man with a broken tooth smiled at us. Manuel shot the face and repeatedly fired into the room. Bullets whizzed from the room into the hallway. I gripped my gun but Manuel and Jerome stood in my line of fire. They sprayed more bullets into the room. Manuel leaped through the doorway. More shots, a scream. My ears buzzed from the sharp explosions. A flash of adrenaline shot through my spine. Jerome looked at me and I nodded.

We rushed into the room—a layer of gun smoke floated at eye level. Manuel slumped against a chair, blood seeping from his belly. Four other bleeding men sprawled in awkward positions. Blood pooled on the floor and spotted the low ceiling.

We did a quick scan of the bloody scene. A golden box sat on a table in a corner of the room. Embossed angels adorned the lid.

Jerome grabbed an iron bar sitting on a shelf. He pounded the lock and the lid sprung open. The box was empty.

Jerome checked Manuel, shook his head and motioned with his gun toward the door. He dashed from the room. I followed as fast as I could. We jumped over Salvador's body and scrambled up the stairs.

The narrow stairwell closed in around us. Jerome puffed and wheezed in front of me, and occasionally muttered a curse. Air erupted from my lungs in shallow and hot bursts. The walls, covered with peeling gray paint, bounced and exaggerated the sounds we made. Repeating bursts of an alarm bell rang up and down the stairwell. Jerome swung open a door and we rushed through to the first level of the parking lot.

Sirens blared. I heard shouting, doors slamming, men running. My knees ached from racing through the stairs. Somewhere along the way I had scraped my elbow. I rubbed the bone to get feeling back in my arm. Exhaustion overwhelmed me and I quit running. We dropped our guns, collapsed on the concrete and waited for the cops. We didn't wait long.

20

I landed in a purgatory of city cops, federal agents, all sizes of jail cells and more cops. Denver detectives, including my old friends Reese and Robbins, interrogated me for hours. When they weren't insulting me, rude teams from the FBI and Homeland Security took over, dead set on nailing me for terrorism.

They kept me isolated from other prisoners and allowed no visitors. I asked for a lawyer, or to talk with Jerome, or make a call to my sister Maxine—everything denied.

I repeatedly demanded info about Corrine and Isabel. The cops looked at one another as though they had a dark secret they were busting a gut to tell me, but they only shrugged their shoulders or rolled their bloodshot eyes and made me feel like I was the dumbest human being on earth.

The cops explained they could keep me under wraps because of the Patriot Act and, as Robbins put it, "Who gives a shit about you, anyway?"

I lost track of time and drifted in a fuzzy, gray awareness. Although exhausted, I did not sleep. I craved water but I couldn't eat much. A candy bar and a bag of peanuts kept me going. A trio of cops wearing bullet-proof vests moved me from one government building to another, at night, and the only constant was that no one believed my story.

I told all of them the truth. At least, as much of the truth that I had to reveal to protect myself. My story was clean and uncomplicated. Four of us had been kidnapped by Lorenzo Ortiz's gang. They forced Jerome and me to participate in the hotel robbery because of threats made against Corrine and Isabel. The gangsters killed each other. I didn't fire a shot. I didn't know about terrorism or smuggled drugs or Mexican cartel warfare. I had no idea why they picked us. I never saw the religious relic. I explained the importance of Juan Diego's vision of the Virgin Mary on a rocky cactus-covered hill near Mexico City and the legend of the miraculous transformation of his cloak. The cops groaned, shook their heads and told me to quit the fairy tales.

I trusted Jerome told the same story. He had no reason to lie. He could be accused of nothing more than contributing his share of bullets, in self-defense, when Manuel started the carnage by shooting Salvador. Jerome really was an innocent bystander.

I used the few and rare minutes on my own, away from the hot lights and bad breath of my interrogators, to think about the many mistakes I had made on the path that led me to the bloody hotel basement. Artie stood at the center of several concentric circles of misery that included Misti and Lorenzo Ortiz, my sisters, Isabel and Jerome. They were all involved, but Artie had set the play in motion and I kept it going with my ill-advised moves against the Butcher. I carried a truckload of remorse.

I hated the intense light in the interrogation room. I developed a headache that split my forehead like a butcher knife. My back ached like someone kicked me in the kidneys. Small black dots danced on the periphery of my vision.

Reese slammed his palms together after the twelfth time he heard my version of what happened.

"It's all bullshit, Gus," he shouted in my face. "You're not telling us why any of this happened." Robbins tapped him on the shoulder, he straightened up and switched to a softer tone. "Why would these cartel guys force you to take part in their double-cross? It doesn't make sense. Why would they bother to snatch the women just to get you and your buddy in the shootout? What's the connection between Ortiz and you?"

"Ortiz used us so he wouldn't have to rely on his men," I said. "He was ripping off the gang, he didn't know who he could trust and he was willing to waste Manuel and Salvador. He grabbed us out of the blue. We were expendable and by using us he saved his men for another day. That's all I can make of it."

"There were six dead Mexicans in the basement of the hotel, Gus, including one of Ortiz's most trusted lieutenants, Manuel Guzmán." Reese pointed out the obvious. "Yet, you and your buddy are still kicking. You see why your story doesn't hold up?"

"I don't know what else to tell you."

"The only thing I can figure is that you're tied to them," Reese said. "Much closer than you're telling us. You got a history with Ortiz you don't want us to find out about?"

I shook my head.

"It goes back to your dead pal Artie Baca. Ortiz is connected to that, and he got you to be his mechanic for the hit."

"That's crazy. I'm not a hit man."

"He didn't pick you and your buddy off the street, cold. You're part of his gang. That's the only logical conclusion. You guys did the dirty work for Ortiz in the hotel basement but because we busted you before you got away you think you can lay it all on him? You want to pin this lame excuse of a story totally on him and his boys? What's going on, Gus?"

The stress and fatigue caught up to me. I started to believe what the police told me. I could be mixed-up with Ortiz, deeper than anyone imagined. I knew men would die, but I followed Ortiz's orders. Maybe I did have secrets the cops needed to know.

I caught myself before I said anything too brainless. I was a pawn in a sick sport devised by Ortiz and his strange sister, and Artie Baca was one of the collateral victims. I remembered Artie, and what happened to him, and I regained my balance.

"I could use a glass of water," I said to Reese.

He cussed in disgust.

I repeated my story, line for line, detail for detail. Reese stormed out of the room.

"You're going down, Corral. It's only a matter of time." Robbins picked up where his partner had left it. "We've only just started." The grilling continued.

At one dark point, I told the two cops, "I'm guilty. You know it, I know it." Reese and Robbins shut up. They waited for me to explain. "Now leave me alone and let me get some sleep."

"Guilty of what?" Reese said. "Finish your statement."

"Of being as stupid as my sister thinks I am. Of trying to out-think you guys, when that's nothing but a sucker bet. Of believing that men like Lorenzo Ortiz aren't as bad as they really are. Of letting Artie Baca back in my life."

"None of that's important to us," Reese said. "Especially Artie Baca. That's Plan B now. Baca's no longer a priority, not after the shootout in the hotel. Your ass is in a sling. You're going down for a long time. This is some serious shit, Gus. Not even your loud-mouthed sister can get you out of this."

"My sister takes care of me. She always has. I'd like to see her. Let me call her." I slurred my words and my hands shook. A coughing fit bent me over. My eyes watered. Reese and Robbins huddled together.

"We're taking a break, Gus," Robbins said. He handed me a bottle of water. "Get some sleep, if you can. We'll get back to this in an hour or so. You're losing it. Think about where you are and how hopeless it is. Save yourself more grief and admit what you were doing in that hotel, and your link to Ortiz. That's all we need. Give us that, it's not much when you think about it, and we'll take care of you. We want bigger fish. We need to close the circle, that's all. Think it over."

They left me alone but I didn't fall asleep. I paced around the small room and thought about Max and her latest girlfriend and how happy they looked at the bar talking about their music. I remembered the smug look on Corrine's face when I returned Pancho Villa's stolen skull. I made a mental note to thank Sylvia for the job, meager as it was. I tried to imagine Reese and Robbins drinking beer in a back yard, grilling hamburgers. Two good old boys enjoying the weekend.

When the cops returned I repeated my story, which happened to be the truth, and made sure they understood I was not any kind of terrorist.

This went on for three days.

The cops complained about my smell and they made me change the jail house orange overalls I had worn since my arrest. I asked for a shower but that got no response.

In the middle of another endless interrogation destined for nowhere, without telling me what was happening, a district attorney paraded me in front of a judge who set bail at $75,000, and the police dumped me in a county jail cell. They told me to call anyone I wanted. The FBI did not say goodbye. Reese and Robbins let loose with a string of "goddams" and "motherfucks" and "hell noes." They almost threw up when they read the lightweight charges filed against me.

Contrary to Reese, my loudmouthed sister did get me out of the mess. The change happened when Corrine's and Isabel's stories exploded in the press and online. They were heroines, brave women who escaped the clutches of notorious Mexican criminals. They were called modern-day Calamity Janes, Wonder Women, even Joan of Arcs—women who faced torture and death and came out on top against very bad men. The cops were forced to realize that I'd been telling the truth and my arrest would not make their careers. Far from a terrorist, I turned out to be a run-of-the-mill lowlife mixed up in something way over his head, more target than thug. Videos of Corrine's press conference went viral and I rode out of jail on the wave of her popularity.

The prosecutor rigged up state charges against me for firearms and conspiracy and a few other crimes that didn't amount to much, at least in the eyes of Paul Reese and Frank Robbins, but none of the law enforcement types had the guts to lower the hammer on me for the dead men in the hotel basement, especially after the women's stories were aired and the entire country heard how they had been tormented, threatened and roughed-up. Daily stories of the continual and gruesome cartel violence in Mexico and along the border transformed Corrine and Isabel into twenty-first century heroines. Corrine gagged at the thought of being portrayed as a defender of the border against illegal brown hooligans.

"Ironic," I told her when I had the chance.

But no reporter would make a hero out of me, and Jerome kept out of the spotlight as much as he could. All he wanted was to go back to running his coffee shop. Jerome and I didn't fit the mold of crusading vigilantes that the reporters and politicians were looking for, and that was okay with me. Corrine milked it, of course. Because her story helped set me free and stopped the interrogations, I wished her more power and all the publicity she wanted.

I had to deal with the charges, which meant hiring a lawyer. On Corrine's advice I turned to a guy I had known since way back, Luis Móntez. He had practiced law in Denver for years. He hung his shingle back when all the Chicano lawyers knew one another on a first-name basis, and he had a lot of experience dealing with guys like me. I trusted him. I had friends who had relied on Móntez and had not been disappointed.

He met me in the jail and carefully listened to my story.

"That's amazing," he said. "I'm not sure I believe it all, but my job is to get you out of here and then make sure you get a fair trial. Neither necessarily requires that I believe you."

"Thanks, that's reassuring."

The first thing he did on my behalf was to convince Sylvia that she should put up her house and business as collateral for my bail. That was a miracle and Móntez impressed me from the jump.

"Sylvia says she will personally cut off your balls if you do anything to jeopardize her shop," he told me when I walked out of the jail.

"I expected no less. I'm surprised she didn't ask for one of my cojones as collateral on her collateral. You must be quite the talker, Móntez."

"I'll take the credit, but, and I shouldn't say this, it wasn't that difficult to get her to agree. For whatever reason, that woman wanted to help. I won't say she's still got a thing for you, but there's something."

The wrinkles around his eyes shrunk into tight circles and his gray mustache stretched around a gold-toothed smile. He gave me a good feeling and I started to believe in my lawyer and the case for Jerome and me.

When I finally made it home, Corrine waited with a volatile mix of anger and relief and frustration. She hollered for an hour or so, even threw a punch at me and broke a plate in disgust. Then she cried, hugged me and broke down. She tried to talk but the words wouldn't come and only the tears flowed free. I put my arms around her and held her. She let out all she had been forced to keep inside for days. After a few minutes she stopped crying and finally explained what had happened to her and Isabel. It was classic Corrine.

21

Corrine told me a story that made sense only because it was Corrine's. She had always been my super sister and the way she outsmarted the cartel goons proved again that she had the courage of a crazy Aztec and the cunning of Old Man Coyote.

"I was pretty sure they were going to kill us," she began. "Isabel knew it, too."

She wanted to rush through the story and get it over with as quickly as possible.

"Give me all the details," I said. "I only know what I saw on the news. That's not enough." I wanted it all, and I believed she needed to tell me everything.

She took deep breaths and calmed down. "But we had other ideas."

That morning, while Jerome and I were carted away to what everyone assumed was our certain deaths, Corrine and Isabel decided that they would not make it easy for Ortiz's killers.

"I'm not letting these pigs touch me or hurt me," Corrine whispered to Isabel. "They're going to have to kill me first. Then I won't care what they do."

"I'm sure you being dead won't change their minds about what they want to do to you," Isabel said.

"We have to go for it," Corrine said. "Whenever we get a chance. These cranked-up machos won't expect too much from two scared women, so we have to use that against them."

"You think we can do it?"

Corrine hesitated. "Not really, but we have to try. What else we got?"

Isabel nodded.

They watched Manuel lead Jerome and me into another room in the building. They assumed that likely was the last time they would see either of us alive.

A short man with stringy hair tied the women's hands behind their backs. The other men called him Inti. He shoved Isabel into the front seat of a white sedan—something expensive with leather seats and very dark tinted windows. Then he pushed Corrine into the rear seat.

Lorenzo Ortiz appeared from the shadows. He leaned into the car's open window and spoke to Inti.

"All you have to do is take these two to the house on Fox. You know which one I mean?"

"Yeah, boss. Where I spent the night. I take the women there, wait for you or Enrique, then you finish it. I make sure they get to the house and stay there. It's only that uh . . . "

"What, puto?"

"I only wish that we could put them in the trunk."

Ortiz slapped him on the forehead. "You know we can't. Just do your job. I should send someone else with you but everyone has a job to do with the tilma, when we get our hands on it. You can handle the two bitches, right? Don't make me regret this, Inti."

Inti picked up his gun and let Lorenzo see it.

"It's under control, boss. Don't worry."

"I do worry, that's my job. Go straight to the house. Don't try to have any fun with them on the way. I don't want a scratch on them. Get them to the house safe and in one piece. That way I'll know you didn't fool around. Understand?"

"Yes, boss. I got it. I'll take care of it."

Lorenzo grabbed Inti's left earlobe and tugged. He pinched until Inti grimaced in pain.

"You'll eat your balls if you don't."

Inti drove without speaking to the women. His gun rested on the seat between his legs. A card with a picture of the Virgin Mary dangled from the rearview mirror. After a few miles he turned on the radio and soon he was humming and shaking his head to brassy banda music. Occasionally he talked on a cell phone.

Corrine understood him to say that everything was all right. The women were quiet and he was almost to the house. He would be on time, with the "merchandise," according to the plan.

Corrine saw that her door was not locked.

Isabel appeared to be asleep. Her dress had ridden up her thighs and Inti couldn't keep his eyes off her legs.

"Inti," Corrine said from her twisted position in the back seat. "Inti," she repeated when the man did not answer. "We haven't eaten for days. We're starving. Can't we get something to eat? Anything, even a burrito or a hamburger. We don't care. We need something. Please, in the name of Our Blessed Lady, our Holy Mother." She spoke in Spanish.

Inti looked surprised but he shook his head. "I'm not crazy," he said. "I have to deliver you two at the house, without delay. If I'm late, Lorenzo will kick the shit out of me."

"It won't take five minutes. Turn into a drive-through and order something to go. What can it hurt? We're tied up. You talk to the order box. It'll be over in minutes. Not even five minutes."

He didn't bother to answer.

"How about something to drink?" Isabel stirred and shook herself. "I feel like I'm going to pass out." Isabel spoke in English but Inti understood her. "I really need some water. I'm dizzy. I might have to throw up."

"Ah, la güerita finally speaks. You thirsty, baby?" He laughed as though he had just cracked the funniest joke he had ever heard.

"Yes. I need water. We haven't had any since . . . " Her voice faded and she slumped against her seat.

"She's in trouble, Inti," Corrine said. "She's dehydrated, weak, thirsty and hungry. She's got diabetes and needs medicine. What if she dies before you get her to Lorenzo? How will that go over with your boss? He'll hold you responsible. You guaranteed that you would get us to the house okay. Isabel's had a rough couple of days. She might not last. All she needs is something to drink."

She saw Inti frown in the mirror.

Isabel moaned.

"She's not doing so good, Inti. There, look. A McDonald's on the left. Get her something to drink. Please."

Isabel moaned again. She coughed and rolled on her seat.

Inti wavered. He slowed the car, almost to a stop. The picture card of Mary swung in the early morning light. He couldn't decide.

"Inti?" Corrine said.

Isabel moaned.

A loud honk bleated from the car behind. All three jumped. Inti jerked against his seat belt. He swerved into the drive-through lane—too fast, too sudden. He slammed the brakes inches from the rear of the car ahead of him in the line.

Corrine heard the gun slide off the seat and clatter to the floor. She bent her body and with her hands behind her jerked open the door and rolled backwards and sideways out of the car.

She tumbled on the asphalt, scraped her knees and banged her forehead.

She hollered. "Help! Police! Help!"

She struggled to her knees, still shouting at the top of her lungs. Horns honked, men shouted. A child cried.

Inti tried to maneuver out of the drive-through lane but a car sat behind him, squeezed up against his rear bumper. He twisted the steering wheel to the right, stomped the gas pedal and slammed into a white pickup with a Mexican flag decal in the window. A tall man with a large belly who wore a brown Stetson jumped out of the small truck. He glared at Corrine, then slapped his palms on the passenger window. He stopped when he saw Isabel's face. He opened the door and she tumbled out, landing on his boots.

Inti jumped from the car and made a run for it. The cowboy in the Stetson moved faster than Corrine expected. He tackled Inti near the bicycle rack and the two men flew and rolled into the metal tubing. Blood spurted from a cut on Inti's arm. The cowboy stood up, dazed but not bleeding. Inti sprawled, unconscious. Corrine continued to scream until one of the McDonald's employees assured her that everything was all right. In minutes, police cars filled the parking lot, paramedics loaded Corrine and Isabel into an ambulance and uniformed cops handcuffed Inti.

The trunk lid of Inti's car popped open in the crash. Four suit-cases filled the trunk. When the police opened the luggage they found bags of heroin, cocaine, marijuana and money, and a box of handguns and bullets.

The fast food manager gave the Durango vaquero a free Big Breakfast and three Happy Meals for his kids. The cowboy drank coffee, talked with the police and waited for a tow truck.

22

I had too much to think over in the days following the shootout. The death and blood and terror turned me into a thinker, something no teacher ever accomplished. I felt responsible for what Corrine and Isabel had gone through and for the mess I made of Jerome's life. Hell, I felt sorry about Manuel—he did what he could to help and all it meant for him was an epitaph for another dead cartel thug.

My sick conscience bothered me most about Misti Ortiz. As far as I knew she was alive, even if she had to live with her crazy brother. She gave us hope when it looked like we were finished, and though her motive may have been simple—blood simple—she took a risk for us without any expected pay-off except the slim chance that one of us might kill her brother. Had Lorenzo figured out that she'd slipped us a gun? Was she paying the price for the totally screwed-up outcome of his outrageous plan? Was there something I should do for her?

I played around with the idea of calling her or trying to see her, but it didn't take long to conclude that was a dumb move, for her and me. I stalled and my guilt trip ended where it started, nowhere.

I tried to hide out after my release. I knew Lorenzo Ortiz would come after me. He needed his payback the way other men needed water, and I seriously thought again about running away.

Shoe helped with that problem. He stopped by the shop. I hesitated before I finally let him in the back door.

"I guess you can relax now," he said.

"Really? Why's that?"

"Ortiz has left the building. Word is that he's back in Mexico, running from the feds, his old gang, even the pope's cops. No one's heard from him since the mess at the Majestic. His club and restaurants are closed. All of his real estate deals are canceled. No one is taking care of business. He's gone, Gus. He's probably dead by now. He double-crossed the wrong people and it finally caught up to him."

"I won't believe it until I see him stretched out in his coffin."

Shoe laughed and eventually he convinced me that we should at least get a beer to celebrate. I agreed, but I didn't feel all that good about it.

We walked a couple of blocks over to Pirandello's, a bar we hadn't visited in years. During the walk we talked about the North Side.

I told him I resented the new people, the new buildings, the increased traffic and the expensive restaurants. I cursed everything and everyone that was new. I felt bitter and suspicious. I could blame that on Lorenzo Ortiz.

"You know, I think I like it, Gus," Shoe said.

I let it go. There was nothing I could do about it and Shoe had a right to his opinion.

"You can take me out to dinner one of these nights. Show off the new North Side."

He laughed and we walked into the bar.

We couldn't remember why we stopped drinking at Pirandello's. The best we came up with was something to do with too many karaoke nights, not that we remembered the nights in that much detail. We finally agreed that it didn't matter.

The bartender looked like she'd seen better days, back when Reagan was president. She asked what we wanted, not with words but with her eyes and wrinkled forehead. She did not smile when we ordered. In fact, she didn't say a word to us the entire time we were seated at the bar. Again, I told Shoe that it did not matter.

The place ebbed and flowed with the dynamics of the neighborhood for decades. It offered decent Little Devils—sausage sandwiches with green chile strips. The beer was always cold. We recalled nights when beer pitchers flew across the room and drunks punched each other in the restrooms. We talked about those nights for a few minutes. At the time, we regretted being on the scene. That afternoon, Shoe and I made it sound as though those flying pitchers and toilet wrestling matches were some of the greatest memories two guys from the North Side could have.

I was relieved when Shoe finally made it to his point. He said how he couldn't even begin to imagine what I had gone through. "Surreal," he said. "The Virgin thing, kidnapped and the way you were forced to try to steal it, and those maniac Mexicans. Surreal. Surrealistic. They should make a movie out of your life, Gus. You have to tell me everything."

I did—most of it, anyway. Some details I'd never reveal to Shoe, or anyone else. Only Jerome and I would know. Shoe shook his head and pounded the bar with his hand.

When he finally tired of asking for more about the shooting and the guys who were killed, and how Jerome and I survived, I asked him about what I wanted to know.

"What are people saying about me now that most of the story's gone public?"

"Well, everyone's surprised by Corrine, you can guess that. But then, no one is, if you know what I mean."

"Yeah," I said. "I know what you mean. That's Corrine."

"An original, one-of-a-kind. Only on the North Side."

We raised our glasses to Corrine.

"How about me?" I asked. "Anyone say anything about the mess I made of things, about how I almost got my sister killed?"

Shoe looked at me over the rim of his glass of beer. "You're kidding, right? No one talks like that. Least, no one I know, or anyone who knows you. You did what you had to do. Those guys were insane, crazy insane. I think most people believe you handled it pretty good, Gus. You and Jerome. Some of the boys told me they didn't think you had it in you. They mean it in a good way."

"I don't know why I even care. But I'm tripping on what people think. I should get over it."

"That's right. Move on, bro. You and Corrine and Jerome made it out alive. Isabel, too. Now, that's someone you should make amends to. Talk about being in the wrong place at the wrong time.

All those years she doesn't have any contact with you, then she hooks up with you for one night, and the next thing, she almost ends up shot and who knows what else by cartel hitters. You ought to deal with her, Gus. That would be my recommendation."

Shoe was right. We finished a few more beers, then he took off. I walked back to the shop where I thought about Isabel for a long time. Isabel suffered the brunt of Lorenzo's brutality and all because of a one-night stand that we both forgot about almost before the night was over.

The next day I gave her a call and she agreed to meet me for a late lunch, reluctantly, for sure, but she said that we needed to wrap things up. She used the word "closure." I began to believe that Lorenzo Ortiz was gone from my life and I could do things like lunch dates.

She picked Gaetano's and that was okay with me. I could always be talked into sausage, peppers and spaghetti.

The restaurant had a colorful, but seedy history. The Smaldone family had owned the place for years and used it as a center for illegal gambling. According to Denver tradition, the Smaldones were one of the few crime families operating out of Denver, back when "crime family" meant La Cosa Nostra, wise guys and goodfellas. That part of the story was over, but the place still looked like a mobster's clubhouse. Dark woods and fancy wallpaper covered the walls. Italian love songs or opera solos played in the background. Frank, Dino and Sammy smiled from the walls. A sign near the cash register glamorized Rat Pack culture. The menu hadn't changed in decades.

Isabel looked good, considering all that she had been through. She always bounced back from whatever teenaged trauma she endured as a kid. The security and confidence were still there. My luck with women had been nothing but bad, so spending time with one of my high school dream lovers was an unexpected but pleasant surprise. At least it looked that way after the fact. She rushed out of my bed in the morning like the mattress was made of nails, and we didn't have any contact since then except for the forced association we endured because of Lorenzo Ortiz. Even so, she smiled when she saw me sitting in the corner booth.

The meeting started off awkward with me stumbling over apologies and questions about how she was doing. She responded with more patience than I deserved. I thought she had every right to rip into me, but she didn't go there. During the meal she tried to minimize the harm she suffered at the hands of her kidnappers. She kept talking, and by the time our tiramisu arrived, she quietly cried and leaned against my shoulder.

"I'm sorry, Isabel. It's my fault. I dragged you into this."

"Those animals weren't going to let anything get in the way of what they were after. If it hadn't been for Corrine . . . " She didn't finish her sentence. The idea of what could have happened to her and Corrine was still too frightening, too raw, for her to talk about.

"Yeah, that's always been the way with my sister. I owe her a lot, too many times. It turned out for the best that you ended up with her. She's the only person I know who could have done what she did to that guy in the McDonald's drive-through."

That image made her laugh. A small, almost silent laugh, but still a laugh.

"One good thing," she said. "I'm writing like crazy. I can't stop the poems. I'm learning the near-death experience makes a good muse."

I hugged her tighter and we rested on one another and let everything else slip away. We didn't speak or move. After a couple of minutes she scooted away and drank some wine.

"It's funny," she said. "We're talking about our nightmare with gangsters in this place that used to be a Mafia hangout."

"Yeah, if you say so. I just like the food. Always have. But even this place will transform. It has to clean up its act for the new North Side. I mean Highlands. Excuse me."

She ate a bit more dessert but finally she put down her fork. She finished her glass of wine.

"I should go, Gus. I have a meeting to get ready for the start of school. Thanks for doing this. It means a lot. I appreciate that."

She stood up. I grabbed her wrist.

"I want to see you again. I'll call?"

She looked out the large window onto the street.

"I can't. Not now. Let me catch my breath, get on with my normal life." She moved her hand away from mine. "I'll call, Gus. One of these days."

It wasn't much, but it was enough.

That week turned out to be my time for tying up loose ends.

When I showed up at Linda Baca's fancy front door, her face told me all I needed to understand. She didn't know I was coming over and I had to be the last person she expected.

Her voice hid what her face revealed.

She let me in the house and said, "Gus. So happy you came by. I've been meaning to call you. I heard about all the trouble. Your arrest. What a horrible thing. Corrine—is she okay?"

"Yeah, Corrine is fine. You know her. Strongest one in the family. She saved Isabel Scutti's life."

She nodded. "Yes, I've always admired Corrine."

That sounded strange since Linda and Corrine moved in completely different circles—people, events and situations that would never intersect.

"The last time we saw each other," she said, "at the new condos. I need to explain. That was so messed up."

"That's one way to look at it. Messed up, with me thrown out because you and your friend didn't want me asking questions."

"You have to understand, Gus. I didn't know what you were saying, or doing, or why you were acting like that."

I looked around the room that could cover Sylvia's shop and then some. "You alone?" I asked. "No Ray Olivas?"

She tried to smile but she didn't quite succeed. She still projected strength and control, but her eyes blinked too many times and her words came out too quickly.

"No, I mean, yes. I'm here with the kids and my mother-in-law, but Raymond isn't here. Why would he be?"

I didn't hear any sounds from other rooms—no TV, music or people talking. I doubted that the kids and grandma were really in the house.

"Just a hunch."

She sat down on the leather couch and made a motion with her hand for me to sit on a multi-colored recliner.

"You want a drink?"

"No, not now."

I waited. She seemed lost in her thoughts without any intention of starting the conversation. She forced her attention back to me.

"Raymond is, was, Artie's partner," she said. "I told you that, didn't I?"

I nodded. "And your lover."

She started to stand up, but her body sagged and she slumped back on the couch.

"I guess there's no need to lie to you about that. Enough people know the truth. You might as well, too."

"I don't care what kind of marriage you and Artie had, or really anything about your personal life."

"What do you want?"

"Your boyfriend broke into my home. He was looking for something, me I assume. I thought you could explain that before I tried to get an explanation from him. Since you and I are old friends and everything."

"I told him that was a mistake. He never should have done that. He could have been hurt, or someone else, or you. He even took a gun. He wasn't thinking. He could have been arrested. It was all for nothing."

"I don't get it. What do you two think I have that you could possibly want? It can't be anything about Artie. Like you said to the cops, we hadn't been close for years."

She grabbed a glass of dark liquid that sat on the coffee table and took a hurried drink.

"Those days just before Artie was killed were strange. A lot of weirdness. Artie told me that Lorenzo Ortiz tried to get in on our

business, that he wanted to be an investor, as he put it. I told him
to stay away from Ortiz, but Artie never said he severed whatever
ties he had to that man. So some of what Ray did came from that."

"That doesn't make sense," I said.

"Like I said, those few days were so crazy."

"But there's more to why Olivas broke into the shop, isn't
there?"

She took another drink.

"Yeah, okay." Another pause. "We were worried that Artie had
set up something to block me from getting my share of the company, especially with Ortiz possibly forcing his way in. We thought
he wrote me out of the business. When you told me that Artie
wanted you to check on me because I was having an affair, I didn't
believe you."

I shrugged. I had made up my story on the spot and hadn't
expected much from it.

"Artie didn't care enough that he would actually spy on me,"
she continued. "Raymond wasn't so sure. He believed Artie knew
about us, and that you were part of a plan to cut out both of us,
Raymond and me."

I shook my head.

"I know, I know," she said. "For Raymond, it was about the
money and the business. It had to be, in his mind. He thought
Artie planned for an advantage in a divorce, and he wanted to learn
all he could about Ortiz and his involvement. I told him I had plenty on Artie, that he could never have any so-called advantage. Ray
couldn't let it go. He told me that Artie might have given you something that could be used against us, or maybe you had
photographs, or recordings, I don't know what. He wanted to find
it, to be prepared, he said. I told him we should leave it alone."

"That's so wrong. By the time he broke into the shop, Artie was
already dead. What could he do to you?"

"With Artie gone, Ray thought you might try something."

"What? Me?"

"We were both out of control. I told you, it was all crazy. Artie
had been killed. A gangster threatened to move in on the business.

You said Artie hired you to check up on me. We didn't think through any of it. Ray just acted."

"If there had been anything, if I had found something, Artie would have confronted you directly. Or he would have gone straight to Olivas. He wouldn't have sat on it." I remembered how quickly Artie's plan unraveled. "If he had time to act."

She shook her glass and her drink swished around the bottom. "Frankly, Gus, I didn't think you were a threat. Ray was uneasy, nervous, and he decided he needed to talk to you. That's what he told me. He thought he could get the information from you. When he didn't find you that night, he realized his mistake and we let it go. I argued that he should stay away from you. He eventually agreed. What could we do anyway?"

"You could have asked me, Linda. I told you I decided not to do anything for Artie. You should have believed me."

"Yes, you're right, of course." She looked at me. "What can I do about it now?"

"Nothing." I was finished with her. "That night at the condo party, you both should have leveled with me then."

"I'm sorry about that, Gus. We shouldn't have treated you that way. I was overwhelmed when you accused Raymond. I was confused. I didn't know what else to do. I only wanted you to be gone so that we could go on. We had a lot riding on that project. I was afraid that . . . "

"That I would embarrass you and ruin it for you and Olivas? Is that it?"

"Something like that."

I stood up to leave.

"Now that Artie is dead," I said, "you've learned that he didn't do anything to jeopardize your share of his business, or what Olivas should get as his partner. Lorenzo Ortiz made his move but Artie kept him out. You learned that directly from Ortiz the night at the reception for the Don Quixote building."

"How do you know that?"

"Artie and I go back a long way, before you, remember? One thing he always talked about was family. That meant something to him, at one time."

She sunk deeper into her couch.

"In fact, and I'm guessing again, I'd say Artie took pretty good care of you and the kids. Right?"

She looked at me and reluctantly nodded. She finished her drink and clumsily slammed the glass on her coffee table. She and Artie had been together for years. That was really all I had to know.

"Yeah, he took care of us. He never knew what was going on between Raymond and me. I guess we fooled him. If only he had been able to fool me just as well."

23

Moonlight filtered through the dirty windows of the shop creating a series of yellow-white, sharply angled squares on the worn floor. I sat at my makeshift desk playing with the computer, waiting for . . . I didn't know what.

I clicked open the Channel 4 website and almost choked on the headline.

"Catholic Church Says Virgin Mary's Image Never Stolen."

I watched the video feed of an announcement by the Archbishop of Mexico City and laughed at what had to be a cruel joke played on Christians and gangsters alike. The archbishop addressed a crowd of church officials and reporters on the front steps of a beautiful cathedral.

"Unfortunately, ever since September 11, 2001, there has been an escalation in the war between the forces of good and evil, light and darkness. This war, always present in one form or another, has new potential for worldwide violence and terror. The Holy Father, in concert with his advisers, other world leaders and holy men and women from all faiths, recognized the need for the Church to take steps to preserve its history and artifacts against instruments of hate. Beginning in 2003, he authorized strong measures to ensure the safety of Church institutions, significant historical treasures and other sanctified symbols and relics of our faith."

I waited for the punch line.

"Recently, the Church and millions of believers were victimized by men who have no understanding of common human decency. Men who have no understanding of how they have harmed and punished the millions of innocent followers of Christ who daily pray to the Blessed Virgin and her Son. But today we can help to alleviate some of the pain that has been inflicted on the innocent. Today, we can clear the air to some degree."

He paused and surveyed his audience from behind wireless bifocals. "We are tardy in making this announcement. We wanted to take care of this immediately after the attack on the basilica. But, we waited for word from the Holy Father, who urged patience in such an important matter. He, in turn, sought the counsel of wise men and women from around the world of the Church. Although it has taken us several days, we are now in full agreement and the Holy Father has authorized me to address the situation of the venerable tilma." The crowd stirred, anticipating the importance of the Archbishop's words. "The sacred vestment is too holy, too valuable to the beliefs of millions to be kept where it could be at risk, as was demonstrated by the vicious assault and robbery of the basilica. Although it pains my heart to admit this, our beloved Mexico has become too violent to take unnecessary chances with sacred objects, writings and teachings."

He sure had that right.

"The men who attacked the basilica, who attacked the Blessed Virgin, who attacked the Holy Mother Church, only managed to steal a copy of the tilma. The actual icon was never out of the control of the pope and his ministers. The tilma was never in the hands of the murderers and gangsters who have soiled Mexico's reputation forever."

I roused myself and stretched my arms. My mind struggled to wrap around the full implications of the archbishop's announcement.

The phone rang. I shut the laptop.

"Gus?" I recognized Misti Ortiz's voice immediately.

"Yeah?"

"I'm outside, down the street. I wanted to be sure you were there, and that you'll talk with me. About Lorenzo, and . . . and what happened."

"I don't want anything more to do with your crazy brother, or with you. You people almost killed me. Not to mention what you've done to my family and friends. Stay away."

She sobbed into the phone. "I understand." The phone clicked off.

I hung up. I shook my head and cursed at myself. Without any more thinking I made my way to the door, opened it and stepped out into the night. I looked up and down the street. I saw her silhouette at the corner. Her shoulders hunched together, her slim figure more like a shadow than a person. I waved at her. She walked toward me and she moved with difficulty. She was hurt.

Cars were parked along the curb but there was no traffic. Lorenzo Ortiz could have been anywhere in the area.

I stepped back into the shop and waited.

Soft perfume preceded her. She took small steps into the light. Her face was bruised and swollen. A stained bandage covered the spot where the silver ring with a turquoise dot had hung from her eyebrow. She clutched a bulky plastic shopping bag close to her heart.

"Lorenzo?" I said.

She gave me a half-smile that was so out of place my heart skipped a beat. "Who else?"

"He found out you tried to help us?"

"Maybe. He didn't really explain why he beat me up. He never explains."

"Where is he?" I wanted her to say that he was in Mexico, on the run.

"I don't know. When I had a chance I ran."

"So, he's here, in Denver?"

"Of course, where else would he be?"

"I don't know. I thought he . . . it doesn't matter."

"He's been hiding, and waiting. It's been too hot for him to show his face. He doesn't have anything left of his business. He blames you. You know that he'll come after you. You do know that, right?"

I didn't want to think about it. "What are you doing now?"

"I'm going back home, to Mexico. I wanted to tell you something first."

She set down her bag.

I didn't know where the gun came from. Maybe a pocket in her multicolored coat. Before I realized what she was doing, she held the handgun and pointed it at me.

"What . . . ?"

"This is Lorenzo's. One of his guns. I'm giving it to you. He's used it to kill at least four men, and that's just here in Denver. The police should be able to do something with this gun, to do something to Lorenzo. Have him arrested, at least. It has to be used by the police."

The gun was useless as evidence. There was no way to prove that it belonged to Lorenzo. I was sure he had never owned the gun legally, and the most it would show was that it had been shot in a murder. But there was no connection to Lorenzo except for her unsubstantiated accusation. I took the gun from her shaking hand and put it on my desk.

She picked up her bag.

I moved a chair into the light and motioned for her to sit down. When she finally stopped fidgeting in the chair she again dropped her bag and lit up a cigarette.

"How will you leave? Lorenzo will have to stop you."

"I have money. A lot of money. Money was never a problem, not even with Lorenzo. I have friends. Enemies of Lorenzo. There are people in our family who would kill Lorenzo if they could. They'll help me. I'm not worried about where I'm going or what I'll do when I get there. I never had the courage to leave before. Now, I don't care what happens." She stuttered and her final words came out in whispers.

"What are you worried about?"

She inhaled her smoke and held it for a second. "Only, only that I won't move fast enough. Lorenzo is already looking for me. I can't think like I should, can't do what I need to do as quickly as I need to do it. I'm giving Lorenzo too much time to find me. By tomorrow I'll be gone. I have to make it through tonight."

The actual motive for her visit became obvious. The gun was a pretext. She needed a place to hide, at least for one night. She wanted me to protect her.

"You think you're safe with me? You could be putting yourself at more risk just by being here."

"There isn't anywhere else, Gus. Not tonight. I need a few hours. Get some sleep, then I'm gone and away from him, forever."

Her eyes closed. She finally sounded like a teenager. Afraid and alone, on the run, the hardcore woman of the streets had regressed. She looked too young to be where she had ended up.

"This is a mistake," I said. "You should run from here as fast as you can."

She ignored me. Her eyes were still shut.

"Come on, then. You can sleep upstairs. I'll stay down here and try to watch out for . . . for whatever."

I carried my cot up the old stairs. I cleared junk from one of the corners and swept the dust into a pile. Then I fixed up the cot for Misti Ortiz. She was exhausted and some of her cuts and bruises looked like they could burst open from the slightest touch. She stashed her bag and coat under the cot and then collapsed on the thin blankets. I covered her with another blanket and left her to her dreams and nightmares.

I sat in a chair in the back room with my spine twisted and a hard piece of wood jammed against my ribs. The gun rested in my hands. My eyes burned with fatigue and the accumulated stress. Periodically, my legs jerked under a worn blanket. My head throbbed.

"Damn," I said aloud. "These people won't let go."

I called Jerome and got his voicemail. I left a message. "Something's up. Call me, right away."

I considered the cops but didn't follow through.

When Lorenzo Ortiz made his appearance, I was more asleep than awake. He slammed open the door and rushed in from the alley, knocked me out of the chair, kicked me in the stomach and waited while I rolled and gagged on the floor. Then he picked me up, slugged me on the chin and sent me flying backwards into the chair.

"Where is she?"

I groaned and pretended that he had knocked me silly, which wasn't too much of a stretch. I tasted blood. I tried to calm myself but I couldn't steady my ragged breathing.

He raised his fist. I said, "Wait, wait. If you mean Misti—she was here, but she left. She . . . "

Lorenzo lifted me from the chair.

"Cabrón. Where is she?"

"No, she did leave. Out the back . . . "

He tossed me back on the chair.

"I'll find her. She's here. No way that whore is leaving me."

He grabbed me and bent my arm behind my back. He kept me in front of him and pushed his way through my room. His ugly breath poisoned the air and his clammy hands gripped like a man holding on for life. When he saw the door to the stairs I cringed. He jerked open the door and made me lead the way.

We methodically climbed each step into the trapped smothering heat. Lorenzo's breathing sounded heavy and tired. I smelled dust and decay. We reached the top of the stairs and Lorenzo held back for a minute. My eyes strained to make out details. The only sounds came from Lorenzo's rough gulps of air.

He pushed me forward.

Although I had cleaned a space for Misti's cot, the rest of the room was as filthy as always. The balcony windows let in dim light that created a haze in the upper part of the room. I couldn't see the boxes, junk and swollen plastic bags strewn across the floor and I tripped more than once, only to be kept upright by Lorenzo's strong grip.

"I told you, she's gone. She's not here. Why would I lie to you? I don't owe her anything."

He thumped the back of my head. "Shut up! She's here and when I find her . . . "

He tripped on a mannequin's arm, his grip slipped and I wrenched free. We both went off-balance and I felt myself swaying back toward the stairs.

The floor creaked in the northwest corner of the large room. Lorenzo jumped and turned to the noise. I took my chance. I grabbed him and started punching his face. He pushed me away and I landed on the dirty floor. When I looked up I saw only the barrel of the gun Misti had given me earlier.

I closed my eyes and waited for the end. The sound of the shot snapped my head but Lorenzo hadn't pulled the trigger. My ears rang and the sulfur smell of the gun's explosion replaced the musty odor of the room. Lorenzo cried out. He started to fall and I rolled out of his way. He landed hard and dropped his gun. I pounced on it. I stood and held the gun on him.

Misti Ortiz emerged from the darkness into a halo of moonlight from the windows. Lorenzo twisted into an ugly knot. He clutched his left knee. Misti's bullet had smashed his kneecap and blood flowed like an open faucet down his pants and onto the floor.

She walked slow and steady to us. She kept the gun pointed at her brother. I didn't believe it at first, but when my eyes adapted to the darkness and dim light I saw that she wore the torn and threadbare tilma across her shoulders like a cape.

The vague image of the brown Virgin Mary flapped around her torso and back.

"Give me the gun," I said, as calmly as I could manage. "He's done. He can't hurt you anymore."

In the shadows and dust of the room I thought I saw her smile.

"He can't hurt me anymore? Is that what you said? You don't know, Gus. You don't know."

She held the gun only inches from Lorenzo's head.

"Well, brother," she said in Spanish. "This is it. I always said we would end up like this. How many times did I tell you that I would kill you one day?"

"Misti, no. You can't." Lorenzo choked out his words. "You won't. Not to me. We both know that. Help me out of here. The money's all yours. The tilma, keep it. It won't do me any good. The thing has cursed my life."

She drew the gun back. She caressed the worn, ancient-looking material that draped her neck. She looked at her brother as though she were examining an injured dog.

"The tilma? You still don't know? What craziness! You never read a newspaper, you pay no attention to anything going on in the world. You and your gang ripped off a fake, a copy that the church hung in the basilica for the tourists. The real one is safe. You really are a fool, Lorenzo."

Lorenzo's eyes opened as wide as they could. He winced in pain and rolled on his side. "What? How could that be?" He saw the cloak. "What is that? What . . . ?"

"You idiot. Men like you are so easy—they'll do anything for a little bit more money, or sex, or to inflict more pain. They all have a price. It wasn't that hard for me to get my hands on your precious shawl. I only had to get to one of the chilangos. I had to pay him, in ways I will never do again, but at the end he did what I wanted. Only today I learned that it isn't the real one. The last laugh is on you."

Large tears rolled down Lorenzo's cheeks. "Misti, please. I need some help. I'm dying here."

"No, Lorenzo. You are not dying. Not yet."

I watched it happen and I didn't do anything to stop her.

Lorenzo's skull exploded. Blood and gore sprayed the floor and Misti, and the tilma. I felt warm drops of blood splatter against my left side. She shot him again, in the heart. She aimed the gun at herself and I finally managed to move. I knocked her down and jerked the gun away from her. She didn't struggle or defend herself. She clutched my hand and squeezed like she was falling off a cliff. I thought she said "madre santa" before she passed out.

The smell nauseated me and I had to sit down. The smell came from death and betrayal and fear and other things that I could never know, just as Misti had said. I didn't know.

24

I sat on the wooden bench outside the courtroom waiting for the clerk to call my case. A film of sweat wrapped around my neck and I told myself it was the lack of adequate air circulation, but that was a lie. I swept my hand across my freshly shaved head and regretted that I hadn't brought in a bottle of water. The wait provided a good time to think about my situation, about the last several weeks and about my luck or fate or destiny or whatever it's called, I was never sure. But then, on second thought, I realized that I would have plenty of time to think about it, over and over again.

That morning, Corrine drove me into downtown. On the way we listened to Max's long-promised demo CD. The Rakers did the best they could with a Jim Pepper song. Not quite the jazz fusion I expected, and certainly not *Bitches Brew*, but the band sounded good. Max's voice conquered the intensity of the instruments and gave new life to the old lyrics:

> *water spirit feelin'*
> *springin' round my head*
> *makes me feel glad*
> *that I'm not dead*
> *whoa rah neeko, whoa rah neeko*

I couldn't have said it better.

To anyone watching me, my predicament might have looked bad, not that I wanted pity or anything like that. I was a convicted felon waiting for sentencing, facing several years of prison time. This turn of events had piled on my otherwise weak existence— working for my ex-wife in her second-hand junk store; no future to speak of; and only a few months before I had been the target of killers who made my life even more miserable. My sister and friends had been kidnapped, threatened with death, and generally under attack because, and only because, they knew me. One of my best friends had vowed to never speak to me again. I had watched men die bloody, violent deaths, and an abused young woman break into a hundred shattered pieces. And yet, the person watching me would have been perplexed, perhaps mystified, because I sat with a smile on my face. A sweaty smile, to be sure, with maybe a hint of a nervous tic, but still a smile.

Luis Móntez had done all right by me, although Corrine and Max had a different opinion, which they expressed out loud and often seeing as how I was their only brother. Corrine had another interest in making sure Móntez did his best. She and Sylvia were covering the lawyer's bill. I guaranteed that I would pay them back, even though it might take a while.

Móntez was worth it. Considering the bodies scattered all over Denver, and that I had played a central role in the events that caused the bodies, I could handle a three-year sentence for the offense of possession of an illegal weapon. Móntez said I should have to do only about nine months with good behavior, time served and prison overcrowding. Not too bad, when all was said and done.

I sat up when Detectives Reese and Robbins headed my way. They were dressed for court, Robbins as spiffy as ever, Reese a little better than his usual used car salesman look. Robbins passed me and I heard him sniff, like something rotten polluted the air, but he didn't stop to chat. On the other hand, Reese sauntered directly to me, stood with his arms folded across his chest and glared. He shook his head.

"You got more dirt that needs to be uncovered, Gus. I'm going to dig. We aren't through, not by a long shot." He did the fingers-pointing-at-his-eyes-then-at-me thing. "I'm still watching you."

"You gonna join me in prison, detective? You and I are done for a while. I'll see you next year."

"You and me have just started. I got something to say to the judge today about you and your pals and your business with Lorenzo Ortiz. Even if your lawyer worked something out, I'm gonna say my piece, and I'll be waiting for you when you get out. Remember that, Gus. I'm waiting for you."

Reese kicked my shin and I doubled over. He turned his back to me and walked into the courtroom.

A lot of good that did him. The deal was set. Móntez had assured me of that. The District Attorney accepted that Jerome and I had been forced into participating in the hotel blood bath in order to defend Corrine, Isabel and ourselves, and no one was all that upset that I didn't prevent the execution of Lorenzo Ortiz. In fact, Lorenzo's death was a big plus in the negotiations, according to Móntez.

"The killing of Ortiz broke the dam. People you wouldn't expect are telling their stories about how the Butcher and his gang did them wrong. So many arrests, it's a defense attorney's dream come true. Even Artie's partner, Ray Olivas, was brought in by the cops, for questioning, as they put it."

"I hope they made him sweat."

Móntez shrugged. "Don't know how that'll turn out. They did charge that real estate guy, Twittle. Turns out he and Ortiz were tighter than Cheech and Chong."

"Everything's copasetic? All worked out? Except for one thing."

"What's that?" Montez said.

"Artie Baca? Remember him? Anyone ever gonna do anything about his killing?"

Móntez nodded. "They all think it was Ortiz, but there's nothing concrete to pin on him. Not about that killing, at least. They know he tried to muscle in on Artie's business and his property developments, and that Artie resisted. They figure that's enough of a motive for a guy like the Butcher. The DA will close that file with a memo about Ortiz. Then it turns into a cold case. It's not complete but it's all Artie is going to get out of the justice system."

"The cops go along with that, too?"

Móntez scratched his mustache. "Yeah, except for your buddy Paul Reese. His file will never be closed on that case, but he's got no leads and his partner wants to move on. He's sick and tired of you. He told me." He narrowed his eyes and stared through me. "Everything's getting hung on Ortiz."

Still, there was too much blood and too many headlines and more than enough Mexican Embassy posturing to let Jerome and me off the hook completely. It came down to another choice for me and I did what I thought had to be done. I took the fall as long as Jerome did not have to catch any heat—and I insisted on a guarantee. Mexico got its half-pound of flesh, the DA could close his file and the world became a better place with Lorenzo Ortiz dead and Gus Corral on his way to prison.

The two cops could squeal and squawk all they wanted. I would do time, no doubt about that, but not for murder, not for racketeering, not for conspiracy to steal the blessed tilma, not even for standing by and watching a hopeless Misti Ortiz kill her brother Lorenzo. No, I was becoming a convict because I had let Mr. Cool, Artie Baca, talk me into his freaky scheme. I told myself that I owed the time I would have to serve, if only for being such a pendejo when it came to Artie. Forget about what I was really guilty of.

I kept coming back to the one inescapable truth—it was all my fault. I was the one to blame for Corrine's and Isabel's trip through hell, the split between Jerome and me, and the Artie thing. All on me.

The craziness started early, the night after Artie visited me at Sylvia's shop when he talked me into acting as a go-between for him and Misti. The thousand dollars had tempted me and I fell for his rap, even though it came off wrong the way he explained it. I jumped over the edge when I should have sat back and enjoyed the view. I thought we worked out our plan to pay off Misti and make sure she understood there was only one payment for her and any attempt to extract more cash from Artie would be met with resistance and cops.

Yeah, so I was surprised when he called me again later that night. He was desperate and angry. I shouldn't have agreed to meet him. And yet, I said yes when he demanded that I come over to one of his projects. I'm not sure why I let him get to me again, like so many times before. That night I told myself that I had changed my mind and I wanted out of my partnership with Artie. I thought I would tell him to find another sucker.

"There are two condos in the building," Artie instructed. "They're not quite finished. No one will be there. We'll have privacy. I'll let you in through the alley door of number 3202. We have to talk some more, Gus. There's been a change."

"It's past midnight, Artie. Can't this wait? This isn't a good idea."

"Now, Gus. Right now. Ortiz is up to something, we have to stop her."

"What do you mean? What could she be up to?"

"Get over here. We need to talk, now."

I felt the strain in his voice through my cell.

"Okay, okay, I'll be there in a few."

I drove over to the new condos, several blocks from Sylvia's shop but still in the North Side. The streets were quiet and I encountered only an occasional car on my way to the meeting. The neighborhood can be like that—quiet and peaceful, or rowdy and loud, and often at the same time, if that makes any sense. Like that night. The sky was clear, the moon was yellow, and yet there was trouble tumbling down.

I walked from my car along a construction fence until I came to a brick sidewalk that circled the condos. A six-foot half-finished concrete wall bordered the path. The section of the wall that was finished had been sealed and dyed to look like adobe. Wooden frames marked where the rest of the concrete would be poured. I followed the path to the back and knocked on door number 3202. Artie opened it immediately. He nodded and quickly turned away, back into the room. His face was flushed and his skin glistened with sweat. His lip looked swollen. His eyes were yellow and his hands shook—no more Mr. Cool. Words flowed from Artie like blood from a knife wound.

"They want in on my business. That bitch Misti Ortiz and some ugly Mexican, her brother. They just left, right before I called you. They came by and the guy slapped me around. He said he could kill me but he'd rather go to the cops because his sister is under age." He caught his breath. "They'll kill Linda and my kids. He wants fifty thousand now, a down payment he called it, and then a payment every week—twenty percent of what my businesses make."

He paced around the small entryway to the condo and rarely looked at me. He spewed the story of his shakedown.

"He said he would get me cheap labor and materials, and take care of permits with bribes. He guaranteed no problems. But he'll ruin me if I don't play along." He punched his hands together. "They said they were coming back for the money, here tonight. That's when we finish them off."

It would have been easy to say, *it's your own damn fault.* "Take it easy, Artie."

"The dirty little bitch. I'll kill her, smash her pretty little face, cut . . . "

His mouth hung open. He looked stunned, overwhelmed. His adulterous fantasy had busted open on him and threatened to sink him and everything he worked for.

"Artie, now's the time to go to the cops. Let them deal with this. You can have her arrested and the threats will stop. It's the only thing you can . . . "

"No fucking way," he shouted at me. He leaned into my face, tight fists at his sides, his jaw bones mechanically clenching and unclenching. I stared into red eyes and a grotesque smile. "You think I'm going to prison because of her? For rape? They have me by the balls. There's only one thing I can do. We're taking care of this trash. You and me, tonight."

He reached into a box on the floor and came up with a gun in each hand. He tried to give me one. I refused to take it. He dropped one gun, grabbed my wrist and squeezed. His grip was hot and solid and he forced my hand open. He stuck the gun on my palm and closed my fingers around the handle.

"This won't work, Artie. I'm not doing it. You can expose them—it's extortion, blackmail. Plus the threats to harm you and your family. You can't . . . "

"Listen, you piece of shit. You're going to do what I tell you to do or your pathetic existence is over. Remember, I know what you did that night we broke into the drug store, I know you killed that guy . . . "

He was wrong but I wasn't about to correct him. In Artie's crazy brain he thought he recounted reality and that his twisted version of what had happened so many years before was the truth. He blocked out that he was the one who killed the bum who barged in on us going through the pills and powders and boxes of drugs.

We were less than a year out of high school and I thought I was desperate for money, excitement or something. Artie came to me with proposals and I went along, including trying to get rich quick with stolen drugs. We thought we were outlaws, desperadoes we called ourselves. It was all a dangerous joke, until that one night.

Artie smashed the homeless guy's head before I could do anything to stop him. I panicked and ran, leaving Artie to clean up his mess. The story in the papers had the cops concluding that two men from a nearby shelter broke into the drug store, argued about the take, and one killed the other. They even found a confused and psychotic man who slept along the banks of Cherry Creek to confess to the killing.

That same week Artie and I were arrested for a previous break-in where we had been caught on tape. We spent a month in the county jail before our public defender worked out a misdemeanor charge that set us both free. We were young idiots without a record, and the take in the burglary had been minimal. Our defender told the judge that we had learned our lesson, that we were harmless, and that there wasn't any reason to think that we'd ever be back in court. The judge bought it and Artie and I were given a second chance that neither of us deserved.

The last time I spoke to Artie before he called on me at Sylvia's store had been when we both walked out of the jail.

"Stay away from me, Artie," I had said.

"Don't worry about that, Gus. I promise you, you're the last guy I ever want to see."

We never mentioned the homeless man. We never tried to explain it to ourselves.

He had kept his promise until the hot stuffy day he walked into Sylvia's Superb Shoppe and talked me into helping him with Misti Ortiz.

Artie stopped his tirade against Misti and me and anyone else who would try to jerk him around. He slouched, almost bent in half from whatever heavy load he carried. We stood in the entrance to the condo, a semicircle of walls that merged into a hallway that led back into the living areas. A bare bulb hung over our heads, and unfinished drywall surrounded us. A pile of tools took up space in one of the corners. Paint cans, rags and oily boards cluttered the floor. The place would be worth a fortune when it was finished but that night it looked empty and minimal, unfinished and cheap.

He picked up the gun he had dropped.

Artie aimed at my left eye. He said, "You have a choice, Gus. What's it going to be?"

He was asking me if I chose to go along with him, again, or to take a bullet. But in that stark light and wrecked space, with the photo of Misti Ortiz swirling in my head, I took it a different way. I thought he offered me another choice. The desperate, pleading look in his eyes emphasized the options. The seconds that turned into hours that turned into years while he held his gun on me and did nothing convinced me that Artie saw that he had reached his end.

"What happened, Artie?" I asked. "How did it go wrong for you?"

He shook his head. "I don't know. It's all gone to hell. My business, my marriage, everything. I'll never survive this . . . I'm done." His hands shook but he kept his gun pointed at me.

"You had it all, Artie."

Light returned to his eyes. "I still do. I've taken care of my family. Anything happens to me—anything—Linda gets it all. She and the kids will be all right, no matter what. Ortiz and her brother can't touch them. I'm too smart for those pigs."

The light went out. "It's only me. Only me."

I slowly raised my gun. He stared at my hand. He slumped even more. His lips trembled. The gun in his hand quivered. Tears and mucus dripped off his chin. He moved his eyes from me and looked at the incomplete walls and the construction debris of his last business venture.

We shared the room with ghosts.

"You can't do it," he said. "It's not in you. You're not me."

"You're right about that."

I leveled the gun and shot him.

I picked up his gun, avoided him and his blood, pushed the door open with my foot, and left without touching anything. I waited a few seconds outside the door. No one approached. A dog barked from the darkness but there were no other sounds except for my hurried breathing and hard-working heart.

I drove a few blocks to another construction site, all the while listening for the cops. I dropped the guns in the wooden frame of an unfinished foundation and prayed that the concrete would be poured soon and the guns forever buried. Then I returned to Sylvia's back room and waited in vain for the cops.

After that I did what I could to throw off the police and get them interested in Lorenzo Ortiz. But Reese and Robbins were determined to nail me, maybe they were too smart after all—they knew something was up with me but they couldn't prove it. My contrived chess moves only stirred up more trouble than I had anticipated, and put the people I loved at risk.

25

Móntez approached. He carried a battered briefcase and he looked old—gray, wrinkled and a slight stoop in his posture. But his smile was diamonds. Trailing him were my sisters, Isabel, Sylvia, Shoe and Ice. Even Jerome showed up—I told him I'd appreciate his visits. He didn't say he would make any but he didn't deny it either. None of them smiled and they looked way too serious. I stood and followed Móntez through the courtroom door.

I didn't feel sorry for myself. I deserved my sentence and more. My sisters and friends didn't agree but they didn't know the whole story.

The homeless guy had started to show up in my nightmares even though that was all Artie. Misti Ortiz was there, too, and I wondered how she coped while a crew of state doctors tried to undo the years of damage caused by her brother. I didn't hold it against her that she already had the tilma when she gave me the gun she hoped I would use to kill Lorenzo.

I didn't know what happened to the fake tilma, or whether it really was a fake. The archbishop's cover story was too convenient for the Church. I promised myself that when I had the money and the time, I would visit the Basilica of Our Lady of Guadalupe and stare long and hard at the mysterious piece of maguey cloth. I'd be looking for stains from Lorenzo's blood.

I had no problem also imagining that the tilma ended up with Corrine, stored away with the skull of Pancho Villa.

The thing about Artie—who's to say it wasn't what he wanted after all? It sure looked like it to me that night at the condos. But then, I'd been wrong before. Only Artie knew for sure and he wasn't talking to anyone.

I focused on Corrine's favorite slogan.

Only the strong survive.